The cockpit door opened and the sexiest man Maria had ever laid eyes on stepped into view.

He tipped his cowboy hat. "Howdy, ma'am. Sorry about the mess I made. I'll cover the damages."

When he grinned Maria swore her heart flipped upside down in her chest. "Who are you?" Maria tried to squelch the fluttering in her stomach; she was too old to swoon over a man.

Riley stepped closer and spread his arms wide, grinning. "I'm a cowboy."

"Aren't they all," Maria said, rolling her eyes.

Amused, Riley tapped a finger against his belt buckle. "Standing before you, ma'am, is a bonafide world champion bronc-buster."

"Don't call me that." Maria's brown eyes flashed with warning.

"Call you what?"

"Ma'am."

Riley winked at her. Leaning in, he whispered, "Everything else that comes to mind would make you blush."

Dear Reader,

What woman wouldn't be thrilled to have the attention and admiration of a younger man? The older woman/younger man relationship is becoming more and more accepted in today's society. There are countless studies attesting to the compatibility of couples with an age difference of ten or more years. But age isn't the only roadblock standing in Riley and Maria's way of a happily-ever-after.

Living in the trenches of Albuquerque, Maria has devoted her life to helping at-risk teens avoid gangs and succeed in school. Maria is street smart and savvy—except when it comes to sexy young cowboys. She's flustered and beside herself when the reigning world champion bronc bustin' cowboy sets his sights on her. Riley sees no problem with him being wealthy and Maria barely getting by. Him being Caucasian and she being Hispanic. Him flying his own plane and she driving a beat-up station wagon. If Maria listens to her heart and not the demons undermining her confidence, she might see that aside from his young, sexy, adventurous spirit, Riley is the man who holds the key to her heart and a brighter future—hers and the teens' she's trying to help. I hope you enjoy watching Riley and Maria struggle to make their May-December romance official!

For information on other books in my Rodeo Rebels series and to sign up for my monthly newsletter, please visit www.marinthomas.com.

Cowboy up!

Marin

A Rodeo Man's Promise

MARIN THOMAS

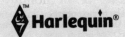

TORONTO NEW YORK LONDON
AMSTERDAM PARIS SYDNEY HAMBURG
STOCKHOLM ATHENS TOKYO MILAN MADRID
PRAGUE WARSAW BUDAPEST AUCKLAND

Recycling programs
for this product may
not exist in your area.

ISBN-13: 978-0-373-75386-4

A RODEO MAN'S PROMISE

Printed in U.S.A.

ABOUT THE AUTHOR

Marin Thomas grew up in Janesville, Wisconsin. She attended the University of Arizona in Tucson on a Division I basketball scholarship. In 1986, she graduated with a B.A. in radio-television and married her college sweetheart in a five-minute ceremony in Las Vegas. Marin was inducted in May 2005 into the Janesville Sports Hall of Fame for her basketball accomplishments. Even though she now calls Chicago home, she's a living testament to the old adage "You can take the girl out of the small town, but you can't take the small town out of the girl." Marin's heart still lies in small-town life, which she loves to write about in her books.

Books by Marin Thomas

HARLEQUIN AMERICAN ROMANCE

1024—THE COWBOY AND THE BRIDE
1050—DADDY BY CHOICE
1079—HOMEWARD BOUND
1124—AARON UNDER CONSTRUCTION*
1148—NELSON IN COMMAND*
1165—SUMMER LOVIN'
        "The Preacher's Daughter"
1175—RYAN'S RENOVATION*
1184—FOR THE CHILDREN**
1200—IN A SOLDIER'S ARMS**
1224—A COAL MINER'S WIFE**
1236—THE COWBOY AND THE ANGEL
1253—A COWBOY'S PROMISE
1271—SAMANTHA'S COWBOY
1288—A COWBOY CHRISTMAS
1314—DEXTER: HONORABLE COWBOY
1341—ROUGHNECK COWBOY
1352—RODEO DADDY***
1364—THE BULL RIDER'S SECRET***

*The McKade Brothers
**Hearts of Appalachia
***Rodeo Rebels

To Kevin—husband and best friend.

This past May we celebrated twenty-five years of wedded bliss! Who would have predicted a few stolen kisses in a dorm stairwell would lead to getting hitched in Vegas and settling into our first home in Phoenix. We didn't stay put long…off we went to The Golden State. Along the way we added two kids and a dog. Then we headed to the Garden State for a couple of years before migrating west again to the Centennial State. From there we planted roots in the Lone Star State, added two more dogs and Taz the hamster to our family before packing up and moving to the Prairie State. This year we finally made it back to the place we began our life together…the Grand Canyon State. What an amazing ride it's been and one I wouldn't trade for the world! But I'm tired. I vote we stay put the next twenty-five years, find us a couple of rocking chairs, kick back and watch our kids navigate life, marriage and children while we grow old together.

I love you, GB!

Chapter One

Friday afternoon, Riley Fitzgerald climbed out of a green Chevy cab in front of the Fremont County fairgrounds in Canon City, Colorado. The late-August sun slipped behind a puffy white cloud, casting a shadow over the livestock buildings. He offered the driver a hundred-dollar bill. "Keep the change, Rosalinda."

"A pleasure, Mr. Fitzgerald." The owner of Canon City Cab was old enough to be Riley's grandmother and just as dependable. On his approach to the Fremont County Airport, he'd radioed the control tower to arrange a cab ride for him to the Royal Gorge Rodeo. "Good luck today." Rosalinda waved then drove off.

Riley slung his gear bag over his shoulder and cut across the parking lot.

"Hey, Riley!" A petite blonde sashayed toward him, her perky breasts bouncing beneath a hot pink T-shirt with the words *Cowgirls Ride Better* printed in black lettering across the front.

Sugar waited tables at Dirty Lil's—a roadhouse where cowboys hung out and swapped eight-second stories. Their one and only lusty kiss three years ago had been a bust, but they'd remained good friends. "Did you miss me?" Riley asked.

"Heck yeah, I missed my biggest tipper." She slipped her arm through his and walked with him to the cowboy-ready area. "You're comin' to the bar later, right?"

"You bet." Maintaining his championship swagger had become increasingly difficult when he hadn't hit a top-three finish since his July 4th win in South Dakota seven weeks ago.

"Hey, Fitzgerald!" Billy Stover waved his cowboy hat. The bronc rider occupied first place in the standings. "Showin' up kind of late in the day, aren't you?" Stover eyed Sugar while Riley signed in for his event.

"Couldn't catch a tailwind with the Cessna." Riley felt a zap of satisfaction at the smack-down. No matter how great Stover became at bronc-bustin', the cowboy would never earn the amount of money Riley had at his disposal on a day-to-day basis.

No sense trying to downplay his wealth when the media made sure Riley's competitors and rodeo fans knew the Fitzgeralds of Lexington, Kentucky, were rolling in dough. He'd heard the whispers behind the chutes—spoiled rich kid had nothing better to do with his time than play cowboy.

After graduating from college with a marketing degree, he'd bypassed the family business—Kentucky Derby horses and a century-old bourbon distillery—and had hit the rodeo circuit, living off his trust fund. Other than sharing a love for the sport, he didn't have a whole lot in common with the average rodeo cowboy. He knew horseflesh—the racing kind—but next to nothing about punching cows, which was what most rodeo contenders did to earn money between rides.

"Forgot you flew your own plane," Stover said.

"You'd forget your brain if it wasn't trapped inside your skull."

Stover spit tobacco juice, the glob landing inches from the toe of Riley's boot. "A win tonight ain't gonna put you back in the running." Listening to the man's crap would be a lot less painful if Riley lasted eight seconds in the saddle. His dismal performance the past month fueled personal attacks and provided fodder for the media.

"Worry about yourself, Stover. Your luck might run out tonight."

"Doubt it." Stover disappeared into the crowd. The sports world was having a field day debating whether or not Riley deserved last year's championship title. Riley's first year on the circuit, he ended the season ranked seventh in the standings. The second year he'd won the title—by default—when Drew Rawlins had scratched his final ride. This year Riley intended to prove the naysayers wrong. He'd had a hell of a run during Cowboy Christmas, but he'd been slipping downhill since then.

"Ignore him." Sugar glared at Stover's retreating back. "Win or lose, you're the hottest cowboy on the circuit."

Too bad Riley's pretty face couldn't keep his butt glued to the saddle.

"Grab a seat, folks, and hang on to your hats." The rodeo announcer's voice boomed over the loudspeakers. "The saddle-bronc competition is about to begin."

"Go get 'em, cowboy." Sugar kissed Riley's cheek then disappeared into the stands.

Rummaging through his gear bag, Riley found his chaps and gloves. He'd put his spurs on during the cab ride to the arena.

"Riley Fitzgerald from Lexington, Kentucky, is up first."

An ear-splitting din echoed through the stands as the crowd stomped their boots on the aluminum bleachers. His confidence might have abandoned Riley but at least his fans hadn't.

"Fitzgerald's about to tangle with one of the orneriest broncs on the circuit."

Riley had ridden Peanut earlier in the season at the Coors Pro Rodeo in Gillette, Wyoming, and the stallion had been hell on hooves. The gelding had practically thrown Riley into the rails. He shoved his Stetson on his head—not that he expected the hat to stay on. Closing his eyes, he inhaled deeply. Large, industrial air vents circulated the smell of horseflesh, urine-soaked hay and sweaty cowboys through the air.

Gotta make it to eight.

He scaled the chute rails and slouched low in the saddle then worked the buck rein around his hand until the rope felt comfortable. As with most notorious broncs Peanut didn't flinch or twitch a muscle—he was every cowboy's best friend until the gate opened.

"You folks may not know that three years ago Fitzgerald won the National Intercollegiate Rodeo Association Championship in saddle-bronc riding his senior year at UNLV. One might recall the story behind that ride…"

The facts surrounding his infamous ride had been embellished through the years until no one believed the truth—sheer luck and not skill had kept Riley in the saddle when Lucky Strike swapped ends—jumped into the air and turned 180 degrees before touching the ground. The ride had vaulted Riley into instant stardom and earned him sponsorship offers from Wrangler, Justin boots and Dodge trucks.

"Hang on, folks. The flagman's signaling a problem with the clock," the announcer said.

A sequence of slow-motion action shots played inside Riley's head as he envisioned his ride. First, he marked out the bronc—touching both heels above the horse's shoulders as the animal exploded from the chute. Peanut bucked, spun and back-jumped. Riley held on, his body moving in sync with the horse while spurring. The image abruptly vanished when loud music blasted through the arena.

"Fitzgerald dropped out of the standings this month. If he's gonna defend his title he's gotta win on the big buckers like Peanut."

Win—exactly what Riley intended to do.

"Clocks have been fixed. Let's see if Fitzgerald can stay in the saddle."

A final squeeze of the rein then Riley signaled the gate man. The chute door swung open and Peanut leapt into the arena. Riley spurred the gelding, goading it to buck harder—the feistier the bronc, the higher the score. But his efforts were in vain. Peanut whirled right, left, then back to the right, but without much vigor.

Son of a bitch. Peanut was acting like a dink—a bucker with no buck.

The buzzer sounded and Riley leapt to the ground, resisting the urge to smack the bronc on the rump as he walked to the chute.

"Don't rightly know what was wrong with Peanut tonight. He sure didn't do Fitzgerald any favors. An eighty isn't good enough for a win. Better luck next time, cowboy."

"Tough draw," Ed Parker said.

Too pissed to speak, Riley opened his gear bag and stowed his rigging. Parker was one of the nicer competitors on the circuit and didn't deserve Riley's cold shoulder; but better to keep his mouth shut than spout statements that would make the morning papers and sully the Fitzgerald name.

Riley's great-great-grandfather Doyle Fitzpatrick had purchased the family's first thoroughbred horse in Ireland and brought the stallion with him when he'd immigrated to America. He sold Duke of Devonshire and used the money to buy Belle Farms—the burned-out shell of a pre-civil war estate on the outskirts of Lexington. Doyle then opened a local bourbon distillery, using the profits to renovate Belle Farms and invest in the world's finest horseflesh.

"You headin' over to Lil's?" Parker asked.

"Yeah." Riley would drink a beer and pretend he didn't give a rat's ass about losing when he did. After socializing he'd phone Rosalinda to fetch him from the bar then he'd fly to his next rodeo in Payson, Arizona.

"I'll give you a lift after my ride," Parker said.

"Appreciate that." Riley headed for the food vendors, where he purchased two hot dogs, fries and a Coke. He sat in the stands and ignored the buckle bunnies with big hair, big boobs and big rhinestone belts, batting their eyelashes at him. Riley's wealth combined with his dark good looks garnered him more than his fair share of female interest. Most of the time, he enjoyed being fussed over but his recent losing streak put him on edge and he didn't appreciate all the female distractions.

He heard the announcer call Parker's name. A few seconds after the gate opened the cowboy sailed over the bronc's head. Parker was out of the running, too. Riley returned to the cowboy-ready area and followed Parker to his truck.

Dirty Lil's was a hop, skip and a jump from the rodeo grounds. They parked behind the building, near a grassy area where bikers threw horseshoes and played poker at picnic tables.

"You ever think about hanging up your spurs?" Parker asked.

Plenty of times. "Never." That's what champions were supposed to say. "Why do you ask?" Riley didn't know much about Parker's personal life other than his father was the foreman of a corporate-owned cattle ranch north of Albuquerque.

"I've been doing this for eight years and all I've gotten for my time and effort is a handful of broken bones and a divorce."

At age twenty-five, marriage wasn't a topic that came to Riley's mind often. His biggest concern was figuring out what he wanted to do with his life. Until then, he didn't dare quit rodeo or his father would demand he return to Lexington and help run Belle Farms. "You have any kids?" he asked Parker.

"A daughter. Shelly's four. I missed her birthday last week because I was in Texas."

Parker was only a few years older than Riley but already a father. Riley figured he'd have kids one day but he couldn't picture himself as a dad anytime soon.

"I don't know about you, but I could use a cold one," Parker said, hopping out of the truck.

A wooden bust of a woman from an ancient sailing ship hung above the entrance to Dirty Lil's. A sign dangled from her neck, reminding customers that Friday night was ladies' mud wrestling.

As far as roadhouses went, Lil's was top-of-the-line and plenty big enough for the cowboy ego. A decent-size dance floor occupied the rear of the establishment, where a stage had been constructed for local bands. In the middle of the room sat a twenty-by-twenty-foot inflated kiddie pool filled with mud. A garden hose hooked up to a spigot behind the bar rested on the floor next to the man-made mud bog.

Waitresses dressed as saloon wenches carried drink trays and flirted with the cowboys. "Hey, fellas." Sugar smiled behind the bar. "Don't stand there gawkin'. Sit down and have a drink."

"Two Coors." Riley fished his wallet from his back pocket. "When did you start pouring drinks?"

"Melanie's on break." Sugar leaned over the bar and whispered in Riley's ear. "Heard about your ride. You'll win next time."

Or the next time. Or the time after that.

As soon as Sugar walked off, Riley chugged his beer, then spent the following hour dancing with a handful of women. He bought a round for the house then caught up with Parker and challenged him to a game of darts—and lost a hundred-buck wager.

"You did that on purpose," Parker accused.

"Did what?"

"Gave the game away."

"You're nuts." Riley swallowed a sip of warm beer. He'd been nursing his second longneck for over an hour. "What?" he asked when Parker stared at him.

"You strut around…a big shot with the women." Parker pointed at Riley's waist. "Flashing your world-champion belt buckle and pilot's license. Buying rounds of beer with hundred-dollar bills."

No sense refuting Parker's charges. Riley was set

for life. He was aware most rodeo cowboys shared motel rooms, slept in their trucks and skipped meals to scrape together enough cash to pay their entry fees and fill their gas tanks. A few guys even set their own broken bones because they didn't have the money to pay for an E.R. visit.

Riley had never experienced sacrifice—that set him apart from the other cowboys on the circuit. In return, his rivals had no idea how it felt to live with the pressure and responsibility attached to the Fitzgerald name.

When Riley refused to debate his privileged life with Parker, the cowboy muttered, "Thanks for the gas money."

"You beat me fair and square." Riley had believed Parker was one of the few cowboys who'd ignored Riley's wealth. If he'd known otherwise, he wouldn't have played darts with one eye closed—his good eye. He couldn't have hit the bull's-eye if he'd been standing five feet in front of the board. He set his beer bottle on the bar.

"You're not stayin' for the mud wrestling?" Parker motioned to the pit behind Riley. Two women wearing string bikinis—pink-and-white polka dot and cherry-red—taunted each other while drooling cowpokes placed bets.

Both blondes were pretty and not shy about flaunting their centerfold figures. Maybe it wouldn't hurt to watch the first match. Riley found a table with an unobstructed view of the pit and far enough away to avoid the spray of mud.

The antique train whistle attached to the wall behind the bar bellowed. Sugar introduced the wrestlers. "Get ready, boys, 'cause Denise and Krista are gonna give you a fight to remember. Both gals made the finals in last year's Royal Gorge mud wrestling competition."

Wolf whistles filled the air.

The women retreated to opposite corners of the kiddie pool and made a big production out of straightening their swimsuits. When the train whistle blew again, the contestants dove into the pit, spewing mud over the edges of the pool. They tussled, slipped and slid until only the whites of their eyes and their teeth were visible. Riley chuckled at the effort the women put into the act. They knew if they gave the cowboys a good show, they'd earn enough money in tips to cover their rent for a month.

"I thought you were leaving?" Sugar sidled up to Riley's table.

"You know me—can't resist a dirty girl."

"You need a real woman." She snorted at the mud-slinging duo. "Not immature, self-centered brats who only want to get their hands on the Fitzgerald fortune."

"And where is a twenty-five-year-old guy to find a mature, worldly woman his own age?"

"Not at Dirty Lil's, that's for sure."

"If I stop coming here, you'll miss me." Riley kissed Sugar's cheek. "I've got to hit the road."

"Fly safe, you hear?"

"Will do." Riley returned to Parker's F-150, where he'd left his gear bag, then phoned the cab company. By the time Rosalinda arrived, thunder echoed in the distance. She stepped on the gas and issued a weather report. Ominous black clouds threatened the skies to the west. At the airport he tipped Rosalinda another hundred before entering the hangar that housed his plane. The *Dark Stranger*—literal translation of his great-great-grandfather's name, Doyle—was a gift to himself after he'd graduated from college.

Ben Walker, the airport operations manager, stood next to the Cessna 350 Corvalis. "High winds and possible hail are headed this way. You're being routed through Albuquerque, then over to Arizona. You've got to be airborne in the next ten minutes. After that they're shutting us down until the storm passes."

"What about fuel?"

"Took care of that earlier." Walker shrugged. "Heard you lost today so I doubted you'd stick around long."

"Thanks."

"Have a safe flight." Walker returned to his office.

Riley got in the plane and hurried through the preflight checklist, then taxied onto the runway. The control tower instructed him to fly twenty miles east then turn south toward Albuquerque.

Once the *Dark Stranger* leveled off at sixteen thousand feet, Riley relaxed behind the controls and turned on the stereo. Time passed quickly and the plane soon entered Albuquerque airspace. He decreased his altitude and veered west toward Arizona. He'd just straightened the aircraft, when out of nowhere an object slammed into the propeller.

"Shit!"

Flecks of blood spattered the windshield and the plane vibrated violently. Riley quickly feathered the propeller and shut down the engine to prevent further damage.

He muttered a prayer and searched for a place to land.

Oh, my God.

Maria Alvarez stared in horror out the window of

her station wagon. The small plane wobbled in the sky, its right wing dipping dramatically before leveling off. The aircraft was losing altitude fast. Maria pressed on the gas pedal as she whizzed along I-40 heading west out of Albuquerque toward Mesita.

Suddenly the plane switched direction and crossed the highway right over her car. He was gliding toward the salvage yard—Maria's destination. Flipping on the blinker, she entered the exit lane. Keeping the plane in sight, she drove along a deserted road for a quarter mile. The road dead-ended and Maria turned onto a dirt path that led to Estefan's Recycling and Auto Salvage. The business had closed to the public years ago but the property had never been cleared of ancient car parts, tires and appliances. The past few months the lot had become the home turf of the Los Locos gang.

Aside from normal gang activities—robbery, drugs and shootings—the Los Locos members were famous for their artistic talent. A recent display of their artwork across the front of an office complex on the south side of Albuquerque depicted an alien invasion of earth. The mural had received praise from the art professors at the University of New Mexico but not the police or the public. Regardless of the gang's creativity, none of its members would escape the 'hood without an education.

Maria was one of five teachers in the city whose students had dropped out or had been expelled from high school. Except for a few instructors, society had written off the troublemakers. Education, not gang affiliation, was the path to a better life. Once the teens joined a gang, leaving alive wasn't an option. Maria's job was to help at-risk teens earn a GED then enroll in a community college or a trade program. Most days she loved her work, but there were times—like now— that her students tested the limits of her patience.

Yesterday, three of her charges had skipped class. When she'd stopped by their homes this afternoon to check on them, their families had no idea of their whereabouts. As she left one of the homes, a younger sibling confessed that his brother, Alonso, had gone to meet the Los Locos at Estefan's Salvage.

As Maria raced toward the junkyard, the plane dropped from the sky and touched down, bouncing twice before racing across the bumpy desert toward the chain-link fence enclosing the property.

He's not going to stop in time.

The aircraft rammed into the fence, ripping several panels from the ground before the nose of the plane crashed into a stockpile of rubber tires, spewing them fifty feet into the air. Amazingly the aircraft came to a halt in one piece.

After parking near the downed fence, Maria clutched the lead pipe she stowed beneath the front seat. This wasn't the first time—nor would it be the last—that she rescued one or more of her students from a dangerous situation. Her father insisted she carry a gun, but after her brother had been shot dead by a gangbanger ten years ago, Maria wanted nothing to do with guns.

Sidestepping scattered debris, she hurried toward the plane. Her steps slowed when the cockpit door opened and the sexiest man she'd ever laid eyes on stepped into view.

He tipped his cowboy hat. "Howdy, ma'am. Sorry about the mess I made of your place. I'll cover the damages."

This past March Maria had celebrated her thirty-fifth birthday. Entering her mid-thirties was tough enough without being "ma'am'd" by a sexy young cowboy. He grinned and she swore her heart flipped upside down in her chest. Embarrassed by her juvenile reaction to the stranger she stopped several yards from the plane.

"You wouldn't happen to have the name of a good aviation mechanic, would you?"

Chapter Two

Stomach tied in knots, Riley walked around the plane, assessing the damage—flat tire. Minor dents. *Oh, man, that couldn't be good*—two mangled propeller blades. Only a bird the size of a hawk could have done that much damage.

Despite a breeze, sweat dripped down his temples as the harrowing descent replayed in his mind. At least his radio hadn't shut off and he'd been able to communicate his safe landing to the control tower at a nearby airport.

"Are you all right?"

The sultry voice startled Riley. He'd forgotten about the woman. He gave her a once-over. Out of habit he catalogued her features, placing them in the plus or minus column. Her voice made the plus column—the raspy quality reminded him of a blues singer.

"Yeah, I'm fine." He moved toward her then stopped on a dime when she lifted the metal pipe above her head.

"Don't come any closer."

This was a first for Riley. Usually, he was the one beating off the women. "I'm no threat."

Keeping hold of the weapon, she crossed her arms in front of her bosom—a well-endowed bosom.

Plus column.

She had curvy hips unlike the skinny buckle bunnies who squeezed their toothpick legs into size-zero Cruel Girl jeans. This lady filled a pair of denims in a way that made Riley want to grab hold of her fanny and never let go.

Three pluses—home run.

"Engine trouble?" she asked.

"Bird strike. I'd hoped to make it to Blue Skies Regional—" the municipal airport was located seven miles northwest of the central business district in Albuquerque "—but I lost altitude too quickly."

"Who are you?"

The female drill sergeant needed to loosen up a bit. He spread his arms wide. "A cowboy."

"Aren't they all." She rolled her eyes.

Amused, Riley tapped a finger against his belt buckle. "Standing before you, ma'am, is a bona fide world-champion bronc-buster."

"Don't call me that." Almond-shaped brown eyes flashed with warning.

"Call you what?"

"Ma'am."

So the lady was a tad touchy about her age. The tiny lines that fanned from the outer corners of her eyes hinted that she was older than Riley by more than a few years. She was on the short side, but there was nothing delicate about her. The arm wielding the pipe sported a well-defined bicep. His mind flashed back to Dirty Lil's—he'd give anything to watch this woman mud wrestle.

"I've never met a real cowboy who wears snakeskin

boots and flies his own plane. My guess is that you're a drug dealer, masquerading as a cowboy."

Whoa. "Sorry to disappoint you, ma'—uh, miss. I left Canon City, Colorado, earlier today after competing in the Royal Gorge Rodeo." She didn't appear impressed. "Go ahead and check my plane for contraband." He dug his cell phone from his pocket. "Or call my agent. He'll verify that I'm Riley Fitzgerald, current NFR saddle-bronc champion." Soon to be dethroned if he didn't get his rodeo act together.

"Agent?" she scoffed. "Is that what they're calling drug cartels these days?"

The lady appeared immune to his charm. Riley couldn't remember the last time a woman had rejected him. Her feistiness and bravado intrigued him and he found her sass sexy. "Why would a drug runner risk landing his plane in a salvage yard?"

"I've seen bolder displays of arrogance."

Now he was an arrogant drug dealer? "As soon as I locate a good mechanic I intend to fly the heck out of Dodge." He removed a handful of hundred-dollar bills from his wallet. "Put this toward the damages. You can send a final bill—"

One of her delicately shaped eyebrows arched. "What?"

"Cowboys don't carry around hundred-dollar bills."

"Take the money!"

Riley jumped inside his skin and scanned the piles of household appliances, searching for the location of the mystery voice. "Who's there?"

"Alonso Marquez, get your backside out here right now." The woman marched toward the graffiti-covered cinder-block hut with broken-out windows and a missing door. The word Office had been painted across the front in big red letters. Rusty refrigerators, washing machines and water heaters sat outside the building. "Victor and Cruz, I know you're there, too." The pipe-wielding crusader halted a few yards before the door when three teens waltzed from the building.

They were dressed the same—baggy pants that hung low on their hips. Black T-shirts. Each wore a bicycle chain lock around their necks and another chain hung from the pocket of their pants, down both sides of their legs, ending an inch above the ground. The baseball caps on their heads were turned sideways—all facing to the left—and their athletic shoes had no laces.

"You guys better have a good reason for skipping class yesterday and missing the quiz."

Quiz? He'd crash-landed his plane, been accused of drug trafficking and now the crazy lady discussed schoolwork with three troublemakers from the 'hood.

"We're not comin' to class no more." The tallest kid of the bunch spoke.

"You're quitting, Cruz? The three of you are this—" she pinched her thumb and forefinger together in front of the boy's face "—close to earning your GEDs."

"We got a better gig goin' on."

"Does this *gig* have anything to do with the Los Locos, Victor?" She tapped the end of the pipe against the boy's chest.

"What if it does?" The teen grimaced, the action stretching the scar on his face. A line of puckered flesh began at his temple and cut across the outer corner of his eye, dragging the skin down before continuing along his cheek and ending at the edge of his mouth. "Hanging with the Locos is better than sitting in class learning stupid stuff, Ms. Alvarez."

Ms. Alvarez was a teacher. Riley didn't envy her job—not if her students were as difficult as these punks.

"Victor—"

"Mind if I butt in?" Four heads swiveled in Riley's direction.

"Awesome landing, dude." The kid named Victor made a fist pump in the air.

"Thanks, but I prefer using runways when possible." Keeping one eye on Ms. Alvarez and her lead pipe and the other on the teens, Riley joined the crowd. "You guys didn't get hurt by flying debris, did you?"

Three heads swiveled side-to-side.

"I'm Riley Fitzgerald." He held out his hand and one of the teens stepped forward, offering his fist. Riley bumped knuckles with the kid.

"Alonso Marquez."

Next, Riley nudged knuckles with the tall teen, who said, "Cruz Rivera."

The kid with the scar kept his hands in his pockets and mumbled, "Victor Vicario."

Riley offered his knuckles to the teacher, but she held out her hand instead. "Maria Alvarez."

Pretty name for a pretty lady. He eyed her weapon. "That's for show, right?"

"No." She smiled and Riley's breath hitched in his chest. She had the most beautiful white teeth and dimples.

"When did you figure out I wasn't a drug lord?" he asked.

Her gaze dropped to his waist. "When you pointed to the horse on your belt buckle."

"I'll be happy to cover the damages if you tell me who owns this place."

"My dad owns it." Cruz and his homies snickered.

"Yeah, Cruz's dad's gonna be ticked when he sees the busted fence," Victor said.

Riley was being conned, but played along. "I'll pay you guys to straighten things up before Cruz's father gets word of the damage." He handed each boy a Ben Franklin. Eyes wide, mouths hanging open, the teens gaped at the money. They'd probably never seen a hundred-dollar bill before.

"Absolutely not." Maria snatched the money from their fingertips. "None of their fathers owns this business, Mr. Fitzgerald."

Mr. Fitzgerald? The only person he'd ever heard called Mr. Fitzgerald was his father.

"Alonso, Cruz and Victor are enrolled in a high school program I teach for at-risk teens."

Cruz attempted to mimic his teacher's voice. "Ms. Alvarez is our last chance to change our ways before we land in prison or fall under the influence of gangs." Laughing, the boys decked each other with playful punches.

"That's enough." Maria scowled. "Get in the car. We'll discuss the ramifications of your actions in a minute."

The boys shuffled off. When they were out of earshot, Maria said, "You landed your plane in an abandoned salvage yard that's rumored to have been taken over by the Los Locos. The boys were hanging out here, waiting for the gang."

"You think the thugs will show up tonight?"

The sexy cowboy pilot was worried about the plane being vandalized. "I don't know."

"Mind if I hitch a ride with you? I need to make arrangements to have the plane towed."

The last thing Maria wanted was a handsome cowboy distracting her while she reprimanded her students. She clearly hesitated too long in answering, because he added, "You don't have to go out of your way. Drop me off wherever you're taking those guys."

She couldn't very well leave him alone in the junkyard with night approaching. "Sure. I'll give you a lift. And I can give you the name of a reliable mechanic."

"I'll fetch my gear bag." He jogged to the plane and Maria had to drag her eyes from his muscular backside.

You're old enough to be his mother. That wasn't exactly true—an older sister, maybe. Regardless, it irked her that a man as young as Riley had thrown her for a loop. With all she'd been through and seen in her thirty-five years she should be immune to a handsome face and a sexy swagger.

"Is the cowboy dude coming or what?" Cruz asked when Maria returned to the station wagon.

"Yep." She settled behind the wheel and glanced in the rearview mirror. The three musketeers sat shoulder-to-shoulder. The boys were all bright and funny, and deserved a chance to escape the gang violence of inner-city life. If only they believed in themselves. Maria was doing her best to nurture their self-confidence and encourage them to study. They had to excel in the classroom if they wanted any chance at a life away from gangs and drugs. The boys' actions today proved that her efforts were falling short.

"We're giving Mr. Fitzgerald a ride into town. You three better mind your manners."

"Are we gonna get to make up the quiz?" Alonso asked.

Of course they would. Maria bent and broke the rules

to help her students succeed. "We'll see." Wouldn't hurt to let them stew.

"C'mon, Ms. Alvarez," Victor whined. "We know the material."

Victor and Alonso glanced at Cruz, expecting their buddy to chime in but Cruz remained silent. Of the three, Maria worried she'd lose Cruz to a gang. A few months ago his younger brother had gotten caught in the crossfire between two rival gangs and had been killed. Maria sensed Cruz wanted revenge. She knew the feeling well, but when she'd attempted to share her personal experience with gang violence, Cruz had shut her out.

"Who gave you guys a ride out here?"

"A trucker dropped us off at the exit ramp on the interstate. We hiked the rest of the way," Victor said.

The passenger door opened and the cowboy tossed a duffel onto the front seat. "Sorry," he said.

"What's in the bag, mister?" Alonso asked.

"Change of clothes and my rodeo gear." He removed his hat and rested it atop his knee.

"Mr. Fitzgerald—"

"Call me Riley." His smile set loose a swarm of butterflies in Maria's stomach.

"Riley," she repeated in her best schoolmarm voice. "Please fasten your seat belt." Once he'd completed the task she made a U-turn and drove away from the salvage yard.

"You ride bulls for real?" Victor asked.

"Nah, I'm not that crazy. I bust broncs."

"You famous?" Cruz asked.

"I won a world title last year at the NFR in Vegas. Ever heard of that? The National Finals Rodeo?"

A resounding "no" erupted from Victor's and Alonso's mouths.

"It's the biggest rodeo of the year. The top fifteen money-making cowboys in each event compete for a world title."

"Does the winner get a lot of coin?" Victor asked.

"Depends on your definition of *a lot.*"

"A thousand dollars," Victor blurted.

"Idiot." Alonso elbowed Victor in the side. "He flies a plane, so he's gotta make more 'n a thousand dollars."

"How'd you learn to fly?" Victor asked.

"Went to flight school while I was in *college.*"

Maria's ears perked at the word college.

"Why'd you go to college?" Victor asked.

"What else was I going to do after high school?" Riley said.

Victor's eyes widened. "You coulda hung out with your homies."

"Yeah, but that would get boring after a while."

The teens exchanged bewildered glances.

"The truth is," Riley said, "my old man insisted I earn a college degree so I'd be prepared to help with the family business."

Intrigued, Maria joined the conversation. "What does your family do?"

"They breed horses."

Her hunch had been correct. "You live on a ranch."

"No, my family lives on a horse farm in Kentucky."

"You don't have a Southern accent," she said.

"Lost the accent when I went to college at UNLV in Las Vegas."

"I'd go to college if the school was next to topless dancers and casinos," Cruz said.

"I was too busy rodeoing to gamble." Riley winked

at Maria and darned if her heart didn't pound harder. She strangled the steering wheel and focused on the dirt road leading to the highway.

"What do you guys do with your spare time?" Riley shifted in his seat. "Are you into sports or clubs?"

"Yeah, we're into clubs." Cruz snorted.

Maria caught Alonso watching her in the rearview mirror. The teen held a special place in her heart—he reminded her of her brother, Juan. Desperate to fit in, he was a follower not a leader. Alonso had much to offer others and she hoped to convince him to attend college after he earned his GED.

"What clubs are you involved in?" Riley asked.

"What do you think?" Cruz said. "We're going to join the Los Locos." The teen acted too tough for his own good.

"Gangs are for losers. Most of those guys land in prison or they get shot dead on the street."

"Gangs are cool," Victor said.

"Then how come all they do is break the law, sell drugs, use drugs and shoot people?" Riley countered.

Maria decided to intervene before the boys went ballistic. "A few of the gangs in the area have unusual talents." She took the on-ramp to the highway. "Members of the Los Locos gang are accomplished artists."

"If they're that good, why aren't they in art school? Or a college program where they can put their creativity to good use?" Riley asked.

"The kids come from disadvantaged backgrounds and—"

"Disadvantaged means poor," Victor interrupted.

"The families can't afford to send their son or daughter to a special school let alone an art camp during the summer months." Maria merged with traffic and headed toward civilization. "Do you know where you want to stay for the night?" she asked Riley.

"Take him to the Lamplight Inn down the block from our house," Victor said. "My sister works there. She'll show you a good time for one of those hundred-dollar bills you got in your wallet."

Riley ignored Victor's comment. "Any motel is fine."

Motel? Maria doubted this cowboy had ever slept in a motel. She'd have to go out of her way and drop off Riley downtown at the Hyatt Regency.

The remainder of the trip was made in silence—the gang wannabes brooding in the backseat and Riley staring at the Sandia Mountains off to the east. When they entered the Five Points neighborhood, Riley tensed. Maria was used to the rough-and-tumble areas in the South Valley, but this Kentucky-bluegrass cowboy had probably never seen urban decay the likes of what he viewed now.

Maria's parents lived in Artrisco, not far from the Five Points, and she'd moved in with them a year ago after ending her relationship with her fiancé, Fernando. Living with her folks was to have been temporary but Maria delayed finding her own place because she felt responsible for her mother's continued decline in health. She turned off of Isleta Boulevard and parked in front of Cruz's home.

The yard was strewn with broken furniture and garbage. The plaster on the outer walls of the house had peeled away and several clay roof tiles were broken or missing. Good thing Albuquerque received less than nine inches of rain per year. Maria unsnapped her belt.

"I don't need an escort," Cruz said.

"I want to speak with your mother."

Cruz hopped out of the car. "You know my mom won't be in any shape to talk."

Sadly, the teen's mother was a methamphetamine addict—all the more reason to make sure Cruz stayed away from gangs and earned his GED. "Promise you'll attend class on Monday."

"Yeah, okay."

"Cruz," Maria called after him.

"What?"

"Be a man of your word."

After Cruz entered the house Maria spoke to Victor and Alonso. "I want you guys to keep your distance from the Los Locos. And both of you had better be ready to take that quiz on Monday."

The boys didn't register a protest as Maria drove them home—two blocks from Cruz's house.

"Thanks for the ride," Alonso said when he got out of the car.

"See ya." Victor followed Alonso into his house.

Maria left the Five Points and made her way toward the river. She drove across Bridge Boulevard then turned on Eight Street. "The Hyatt Regency is on the other side of the Rio Grande."

"Do you do this all the time?" Riley asked.

"Do what?"

"Drive through questionable neighborhoods?"

"Yep. Comes with the job." She also lived in one of those *questionable* neighborhoods Riley referred to. She turned on Tijeras Avenue then stopped in front of the hotel.

Riley faced her, his mouth curving. Maria swore she'd have to ingest a dozen bottles of antacid medicine before her stomach recovered from her run-in with the flying cowboy.

"Let me buy you dinner as a thank you for helping me today," he said.

Dinner...as in a date? It had been months since she'd sat across the table from a man, never mind that Riley Fitzpatrick wasn't just any man. He was a sexy *young* cowboy...man.

"How old are you?" She winced when the question slipped out of her mouth.

"Twenty-five. Does age matter if we're only having dinner?"

Oh, God. Maria's face flamed. Had he guessed she'd been thinking about sex? She really needed to get laid. "Dinner would be nice, but I'm not dressed for the Hyatt. How do you feel about Mexican food?"

"Love it."

"I know just the place." Maria drove back to the other side of the Rio Grande and parked in front of a narrow brick-faced storefront with Abuela's Cocina on the sign, sandwiched between a Laundromat and a liquor store. "'Grandmother's Kitchen,'" Maria said. "Consuelo makes great enchiladas."

"Is it safe?" Riley asked, eyeing the car filled with gangbangers at the corner. The guy in the driver's seat glared at them.

"No riskier than the wild horses you ride." Rodeo could be violent at times, but at least the horses and bulls didn't shoot at the cowboys who rode on their backs.

They made it as far as the restaurant door when a gunshot went off. In a move so quick it snatched the air from Maria's lungs Riley opened the café door and shoved her over the threshold, catching her by the waist when she tripped on the welcome mat in the foyer. Before the door had even shut behind them,

Riley had Maria pressed against the wall, his body shielding hers.

"Did you get hit?" he whispered.

Shock kept her tongue-tied.

"Don't move." Riley settled his palm against her hip, exerting enough force to keep her pinned in place. The heat from his hand burned through her jeans, warming her skin. She giggled.

"What's so funny?"

"Are you finished playing hero?"

"*Hola,* Maria." A young woman entered the hallway, carrying two laminated menus. She stared at Riley's hand still attached to Maria's hip. *"¿Quién es el vaquero?"*

"This cowboy is Riley Fitzgerald. Riley, Sonja. Her aunt owns the restaurant."

Riley tipped his hat. "Ma'am."

Ma'am? Sonja was nineteen. Maria snorted.

"Sígueme," Sonja said, disappearing through a doorway.

Maria followed the hostess into the dining room, stunned that a twenty-five-year-old man made her feel as if she were a carefree young girl and not a woman who had seen and experienced a lifetime of tragedy and heartbreak in thirty-five short years.

Chapter Three

Riley lost his train of thought as he drowned in Maria's brown eyes.

"Do I have food stuck to my face?" She reached for her napkin.

He covered her hand with his, pinning the napkin to the table. "No. Your face is fine. As a matter of fact it's perfect."

Maria's cheeks reddened and Riley chuckled.

"What?"

He released her hand. "I make you nervous."

"No, you don't." The denial lacked conviction.

He eyeballed her fingernail tapping the table and Maria fisted her hand. "Why do I make you uneasy?" he asked.

"Besides the fact that you're a complete stranger?"

"Yeah, besides that." He popped a tortilla chip into his mouth and chewed.

"Let's see." Maria held up one finger. "First, you're sexy and attractive."

Wow. He hadn't seen that one coming. "Thank you."

"You're welcome." A second finger rose in the air. "You're wealthy."

"Money makes you anxious?"

"Didn't your mother teach you that money is the root of all evil?"

"Actually, my father taught me that money solves all problems."

Third finger… "You're young."

He'd read the occasional magazine article that testified to the sexual compatibility of older women and younger men. Made sense to him. He waggled his eyebrows. "Youth has its advantages."

The waitress arrived with their meals and the women spoke in Spanish. Riley guessed they discussed him because the young girl glanced his way more than once. "The enchiladas are great," he said, disrupting the conversation.

"I'll tell Aunt Consuelo you approve of her cooking." The waitress disappeared.

"The whole family works in the business?"

"Years ago Consuelo won the lottery and used the money to open a restaurant. Since then, most of her nieces and nephews have worked here at one time or another."

"I hope she kept part of her winnings and bought a new car or treated herself to a vacation."

"No car or vacation, but she did send her only son to college."

"What does he do?" Riley asked.

"He's an investment banker in Los Angeles." Maria sipped her iced tea. "Pablo visits once a year and attempts to coax his mother to move to California, but Consuelo refuses."

"Why?"

"This is where she was born and raised." Maria smiled. "I know what you're thinking."

"What's that?"

"This neighborhood is a far cry from where you were raised."

"True." No sense pretending he felt at home in the 'hood.

"Consuelo can't retire or close the restaurant because she's the only stable influence in her nieces' and nephews' lives. Without her, the kids would be out on the street running with gangbangers. She pays the kids more than minimum wage, but keeps half their paycheck and deposits the money into a savings account for their college education."

Riley had never had to save a dime in his life. Heck, the day he'd been born his father had opened an investment portfolio in his name with five hundred thousand dollars. Today, the account was worth millions. When it came to college, his father had written a check each semester to the university—not one financial-aid form had been filled out the four years Riley attended UNLV. "Consuelo's a generous woman."

They ate in silence for a few minutes, Riley sensing Maria was eager to end the evening. He wasn't. "You like teaching?" She nodded but didn't elaborate. He'd never had to work at engaging a woman in conversation. "How long have you been a teacher?"

"I taught six years of high school English before volunteering the past five years with the district's at-risk kids. The classes are part of the city's antigang program."

"The boys you gave a ride home earlier…were they expelled from school or did they drop out?"

"All three were expelled. If they fail my class, the educational system writes them off for good."

"Do you have the support of the families?"

"Not as much as I wish. We have students who don't

even know who their fathers are and a few with dads in prison or running with gangs."

Riley had experienced his share of disagreements with his father, but the old man had always been there for him; and Riley couldn't imagine not having a male role model in his life. "Tell me more about the boys you're working with."

"Alonso lost his father when he was seven—gunned down by police in a drug raid. Alonso's mother cleans offices at night and works at a convenience store during the day."

The kid's mother worked two jobs in order to feed her family and keep a roof over their heads. Riley's mother had never worked a day in her married life.

"Why did Alonso get expelled from school?"

"He skipped too many days, but he was between a rock and a hard place. When one of his siblings became ill, Alonso's mother made him stay home to care for them so she wouldn't miss work."

"How often do his brothers and sisters get sick?"

"His little sister Lea has asthma and is prone to pneumonia."

"That's too bad."

Maria narrowed her eyes and Riley resisted the urge to squirm. "You really do feel compassion for Alonso, don't you?"

Riley was the first to acknowledge he led a privileged life. He bought what he wanted, when he wanted and without considering the cost. And why shouldn't he? He had an abundance of money at his fingertips. It wasn't his fault he hadn't had to work for a dime of it. Even though he had nothing in common with Alonso and his family, Riley wasn't so coldhearted that he couldn't sympathize with their daily struggles. "What kind of student is Alonso?"

"A good one. Alonso loves to learn. He's smart and organized with his studies and grasps new concepts easily. He's ready to take his GED test but I've held him back because I haven't devised a financial strategy to pay for his tuition at a community college."

"Alonso wants to go to college?"

"He plans to enter the medical field."

"Nurses and technicians make decent salaries," Riley said.

"And the jobs come with health insurance and benefits. Alonso realizes that if his mother had health insurance his sister would have access to better care."

"What about the boy with the scar?"

"Victor is bright, too, but he's very self-conscious of his face."

"Did a gangbanger cut his face?"

"His mother did that to him."

His own mother?

"She attacked Victor's sister after the girl announced she was pregnant—" Maria shuddered "—by the mother's boyfriend. Victor tried to protect his sister and got himself hurt."

"I hope the woman went to jail."

"The hospital called in the cops after they'd stitched Victor's face but Victor changed his story and said he didn't know his attacker."

"What does Victor want to do with his life?"

"He's not sure. All the kids take career assessment tests and Victor displayed decent math skills and an aptitude for electrical work and plumbing but he's not interested in those fields—which is too bad because a local business has offered to employ students while teaching them the trade."

"What's the deal with the smooth-talker?"

"Cruz Rivera." Maria wrinkled her nose. "Like you, he's popular with the ladies."

Riley placed both hands over his heart. "Was that a compliment?"

"You know you're a good-looking man."

"Thanks."

"For what?"

"For calling me a man." Twenty-five was considered young in many minds; but, at every age, Riley's parents had demanded a level of maturity far beyond his years. In truth, he felt a lot older than twenty-five.

"Cruz prefers to use his muscle over his brain. He's stubborn and bullheaded."

"The kid has the makings of a good rodeo cowboy."

"His father rode bulls before he—"

"Cruz's father was T. C. Rivera?"

"Yes."

Riley had heard stories about Rivera. The man had taken the rodeo circuit by storm when Riley had been in high school. But T.C. had thrown away his chance at a world title when he'd gotten into a brawl in South Dakota and killed a man. "Where's T.C. now?"

"South Dakota State Penitentiary in Sioux Falls."

"Was he close to Cruz?"

"Yes. Cruz is his eldest child. T.C. and Juanita have…had four children."

"What do you mean had?"

"Cruz's younger brother by one year was the victim of gang violence."

"Shot to death?"

"A few months ago. He'd been sitting on his front

porch with Cruz when a fight broke out between two gangs and shots were fired. A stray bullet caught him in the chest."

Unable to imagine witnessing a sibling's death in such a violent manner, Riley suspected Cruz's tough-act demeanor was a facade hiding a hurt and angry young man. "Does Cruz ever visit his father?"

"No. Juanita doesn't have a car and she can't waste hard-earned money on bus fare to take the kids to South Dakota."

"How long is T.C.'s sentence?"

"He won't be eligible for parole for another twenty years."

Cruz would be close to forty when his father left prison. Steering the conversation back to Maria, Riley asked, "What do you do when you're not chasing after delinquent kids?" He really wanted to ask if there was a man in her life.

"Nothing as exciting as flying airplanes or busting broncs."

"Have you flown before?"

"I've never been on a plane."

"Bet you'd enjoy the experience."

"Why would you think that?"

He shrugged. "You're a thrill seeker."

"Hardly."

"Sure you are. Your job is one big thrill. You have no idea what you're going to face when you roll out of bed each morning." She didn't refute his charge. "Any brothers, sisters, nieces or nephews?" *A significant other?*

"Afraid not."

"I have one sister," Riley said. "Bree's twenty-eight."

"What does she do for a living?"

"Manages the horse stables at the farm."

"Stables?"

"The Fitzpatricks breed racing horses."

"What kind of racing horses?"

"The Kentucky Derby kind."

Maria's fork clanked against the side of her plate. Depending on their personal agenda, this is where women either pushed Riley away or attempted to get closer. "Our family's been involved in horse racing for generations."

"That explains the plane, but not the rodeo."

Before Riley had a chance to speak, the waitress appeared with dessert. "What are they?" he asked.

"Polvorones. Almond cookies," Maria said.

Riley sampled one. "They melt in your mouth." He helped himself to a second cookie. "When I was in eleventh grade I had the chance to attend the Lyle Sankey Rodeo School—he's a famous rodeo cowboy. I got hooked on the sport." He chuckled. "My father has since regretted giving me that birthday gift."

Maria smiled and Riley's eyes were drawn to her full lips and enticing dimples. "You have a beautiful mouth."

"Good grief, stop that."

"Stop what?"

"Flirting."

"How old are you?"

"You're not supposed to ask a woman her age."

"Why not? Is your age a big secret?"

She scrunched her nose. "I'm thirty-five."

"You're only ten years older than me."

"Only?" She glanced at her watch. "Hurry and finish your dessert."

"Why the rush?"

"I need to check on my mother."

Riley stuffed the remaining cookie into his mouth. "You mentioned that you knew a good aviation mechanic. I'd prefer to contact him tonight. Do you have his number?"

At first Maria acted as if she hadn't heard his question then her shoulders slumped. "Why don't I take you to see him."

Hot dog. "I'll pay him to drive out to the salvage yard and inspect the plane." Tomorrow Riley would lease a plane to fly to the Payson rodeo.

Riley grasped Maria's hand and squeezed her fingers. He expected her to pull away, but she didn't and the longer their skin remained in contact the hotter the heat that raced along his forearm and spread through his chest. If touching the schoolteacher's hand created such an intense reaction then kissing her would be a thrill unlike anything he'd ever experienced before.

She cleared her throat. "We'd better get going."

He set a hundred on the table.

"Is that all you carry in your wallet…hundred-dollar bills?"

Riley moved behind her chair and whispered in her ear, "Would it matter if I said yes?"

Maria squirmed, the movement bringing Riley's mouth closer to her cheek. The smell of lilies teased his nose and he resisted pressing a kiss to her warm skin. He pulled her chair back and she bolted from the dining room.

Riley followed, doubting she'd claim ten years was too great an age difference after he gave her a real kiss—the slow, hot, wet kind.

HANDS CLENCHING THE STEERING wheel in a death grip, Maria turned onto her parents' street. She hoped her father was in a good mood and her mother hadn't finished off a fifth of vodka—a habit she'd begun after her son died.

Maria parked beneath the carport next to her father's Chevy pickup. He'd forgotten to turn on the outside lights. For once she was grateful. The three-bedroom, two-bathroom ranch was in sad shape. Years of neglect had transformed the flower beds and green grass into dirt and weeds.

"This is where the mechanic lives?" Riley asked.

"Yep." Maria led the way up the front walk. She slid her house key into the lock.

Riley grabbed her arm before she opened the door. "Is the mechanic your...?"

"Father." She stepped inside.

A moment later Riley shut the door and flipped the dead bolt. Obviously he'd noticed the neighborhood wasn't the safest. Twenty years ago the area had been crowded with young families and working couples. Once California gangs began infiltrating Albuquerque, the families that could afford to relocated to the suburbs.

"Make yourself comfortable." Maria disappeared down the narrow hallway leading to the bedrooms. She knocked on her parents' door then poked her head inside the room. Her mother's snores greeted Maria and a half-empty bottle of booze sat on the nightstand. Maria returned to the living room. "Mom's asleep." At her age she should be immune to embarrassment, but she was relieved Riley would be spared meeting her drunk mother.

"Dad's outside in the shed." They left through the

sliding glass doors off the kitchen and walked along the brick path that ended at the rear of the property. Light shone through the windows of her father's workshop. "Dad," Maria called.

The shed door opened. Her father wore his favorite cowboy hat—one given to him on his birthday by Maria's brother right before he'd been shot. The brim of the Stetson was frayed and the crown covered in sweat stains. She doubted her parents would ever let go of their dead son—the Stetson and vodka constant reminders that Maria had failed her family.

"Dad, this is Riley Fitzgerald." She spoke in English even though her father preferred communicating in Spanish. "Riley, this is my father, Ricardo Alvarez."

"How do you do, Mr. Alvarez." Riley shook hands with her father. "Maria tells me you're an airplane mechanic. My Cessna suffered a bird strike and I had to make an emergency landing. I was hoping you could check the plane and assess the damage."

"Where is the Cessna?"

"Estefan's Salvage," Maria answered.

"Lucky for me your daughter was out there searching for her students at the time or I would have been stranded."

Maria focused on Riley, ignoring her father's heated stare. Her parents resented Maria for working with delinquent teens, believing her actions sullied her brother's memory.

"I'll pay you for your time," Riley said. "I need to rent another plane from the Blue Skies Regional Airport until the Cessna's repaired. I'll be in Arizona for a rodeo tomorrow evening, but, barring bad weather, I'd return to Albuquerque on Sunday."

The sooner Riley and his crippled plane left the

state of New Mexico the better. Maria hadn't drawn a deep breath since he'd emerged from the cockpit earlier in the day. "Dad, will you be able to inspect the plane before Sunday?"

"Sí." Her father had once been a gregarious man but his son's death had left him bitter and remote.

"Thank you, Mr. Alvarez." The men shook hands.

Back inside the house, Maria asked, "Would you care for a drink?" Call her fickle. One moment she couldn't wait to dump Riley off at the hotel, the next she didn't want the evening to end.

"Sure." Riley sat on a stool at the countertop then ran his fingers through his hair—gorgeous, black hair.

"Fitzgerald is Irish, right?" Maria placed a can of cola in front of him.

"Wondering why I don't have red hair?"

Maria laughed. "Mind reader."

"I'm Black Irish."

"What's that?"

"My mother traced her lineage back to the Iberian Peninsula, which means my redheaded relatives cohabitated with the Indians and through the centuries each generation has produced an offspring with black hair."

"Are you the only one with dark coloring in your immediate family?"

"My sister's a carrottop. Dad has brownish-red hair and my mother's hair is a blondish-red." He chuckled. "As she ages, she goes blonder to cover the gray."

Maria fingered the ends of her dark hair. She couldn't recall when she'd had her hair professionally colored and she was certain a few gray strands were visible.

"What about your family?" Riley asked. "Are you Mexican, Spanish, or a mixture of both?"

"My great-grandfather was a bricklayer in a small town outside Mexico City. He married my great-grandmother there then they moved to the States and became U.S. citizens. My father and uncles learned to lay brick from their fathers but after high school my dad went into the air force. When Dad retired from the military, he hired on at the regional airport and has worked there ever since."

"I bet your grandfather was proud his son served in the military."

"He was."

"If your father would rather not have to deal with my plane, I'll find a different mechanic."

This is your out. Suggest Riley find another mechanic to fix his airplane, then you'll never see him again. The thought made Maria sad. She was too old for Riley and they lived very different lives. But the cowboy was a flirt, and he made her feel fresh and young inside. She hadn't felt this invigorated since before her brother had passed away. What could it hurt if she saw Riley one more time?

"Dad will be happy to help." She glanced at the wall clock. 10:00 p.m. "You're probably ready to check in at the hotel."

Maria wrote her cell phone number on a piece of paper. "Call me when you know what time you'll arrive on Sunday and I'll arrange for my dad to meet you at the airport."

Riley took the paper, his fingers caressing hers. A zap of electricity spread through her hand and suddenly Sunday couldn't come fast enough.

Chapter Four

"Ladies and gents, welcome to Payson, Arizona, home of the Gary Hardt Memorial Rodeo—the oldest continuous rodeo in the world!" The announcer's voice boomed across the Payson Event Center outdoor arena late Saturday afternoon. Over three thousand people packed the stands.

"This here rodeo began in 1884 and hasn't missed a year since." Whoops and hollers followed.

"You ol'-timers out there might recall the original rodeo venue was a meadow near the intersection of Main Street and Highway 87. Back then wagons circled 'round to create the arena."

Riley dropped his gear bag in the cowboy-ready area. As was his M.O. a cab had driven him from the local regional airport to the rodeo grounds and he had less than fifteen minutes to prepare for his ride.

"Hey, Fitzgerald, heard you had trouble with that fancy plane of yours."

What the hell was Stover doing here? Riley thought the man had been headed to Texas this weekend. Ignoring the question about his Cessna, Riley straightened his chaps. "You stop riding for the big money?"

"You oughta know by now—" Stover's smirk widened "—I'm not letting you out of my sight."

Stover had entered every rodeo Riley had since the beginning of the year—not unusual. The serious contenders followed the money trail. Riley had chosen to ride in Payson because he needed a win to boost his confidence and he'd wanted to get the hell away from Stover—the braggart annoyed the crap out of him.

"You tagging along when I head back to Albuquerque?" Riley asked.

"There's no rodeo in Albuquerque," Stover said.

"Who said anything about a rodeo? There's a lady waiting for me in the Duke City." Riley doubted Maria pined for him, but that wouldn't stop him from chasing what he wanted—and he wanted her.

"You're so full of wind you could fly to New Mexico without your plane."

"Jealous?" Riley grinned.

"Women and rodeo don't mix," Stover said.

No kidding. Most cowboys learned that lesson the hard way.

"You go see your lady, Fitzgerald. Have a nice long visit with her."

Maria wasn't Riley's lady—yet—but Stover's words reminded him that he'd better watch his step around the sexy *señorita* lest he forget his goal of winning a second title. "That's the plan, Stover. I'm gonna drown myself in drink and women."

"Rawlins came out of nowhere last year when he should have retired." Stover fisted his hands. "Then you won the title even though you didn't earn it. This year—" Stover poked himself in the chest "—I'm takin' home the buckle."

Riley turned his back on the cowboy and focused

on his ride. He'd drawn a gelding named Blackheart—a veteran bucker.

"We got plenty of ropin', rasslin' and bustin' activity," the rodeo announcer proclaimed, disrupting Riley's concentration. "As a matter of fact last year's world-champion bronc rider, Riley Fitzgerald, is goin' first today!"

World champion...world champion...world champion...

Repeating the mantra in his head, Riley envisioned Maria's pretty face and flashing brown eyes. She had as much guts and determination as a rodeo cowboy. Tangling with delinquent teens was tougher than riding a wild bronc. He worked three or four times a week for eight seconds. Maria faced gangs and kids living on the edge 24/7 and he doubted her record of success was as good as his.

Today, Riley wanted to impress Maria with a win. He didn't understand why her admiration was important to him—he doubted he'd see her after the Cessna was repaired.

"Folks, the action's at gate number five. Let's see if this world-champion bronc rider can tame Blackheart!"

The roar of the crowd faded in Riley's head as he climbed the chute rails. The familiar pungent smell of livestock calmed his nerves. As soon as he attempted to settle into the saddle, Blackheart rebelled, forcing Riley to hop off. Once the gelding calmed, Riley claimed his seat.

After the dink he'd drawn in Colorado, he was ready for a fight and prayed Blackheart wouldn't let him down. Riley squeezed the buck rein, secured his hat on his head and slid deeper into the saddle. *One. Two. Three.* He signaled the gateman and the chute door opened. Riley's body tensed in anticipation then the horse burst from his metal prison.

Riley raked fur—rolled his spurs high on the gelding's shoulders, inciting the animal to buck harder. Blackheart responded to the taunt by thrusting his hind legs into the air. The horse hit the ground then twirled left, right and back to the left again in quick succession.

Eight seconds passed in a blur. The buzzer sounded but the ride wasn't over until his boots hit the dirt. Dismounts were tricky and had to be timed perfectly so the cowboy didn't break his neck or worse—get his head stomped on. Riley vaulted from the saddle. Luck was with him. He landed on both feet, stumbled once then regained his balance.

"Our world-champion cowboy gave us a world-champion ride. Fitzgerald scored an eighty-six!"

"You lucked out, Fitzgerald," Stover said when Riley returned to the cowboy-ready area.

Before he had a chance to refute Stover's charge, another competitor shouted, "Hey, Fitzgerald! Those kinks the press said you needed to work out just got ironed flat!"

Riley chuckled.

"Don't get cocky. Your eighty-six is about to bite the dust." Stover stomped off.

As Riley stowed his gear, his cell phone rang. He checked caller ID. His father. Perfect timing. "Hey, Dad."

"Where are you?"

"Arizona. Tamed a little booger called Blackheart. I'm in the lead with an eighty-six."

"Congratulations. Got a minute to talk?"

"Sure." Riley grabbed his bag and retreated to a quiet corner away from the bucking chutes.

"I've got a potential buyer coming in sometime mid-October. I want you to show him around Belle Farms."

"Who's the buyer interested in?"

"Bonnie-Blond and Sir Duke's offspring. We're expecting the foal early October."

The mare and stallion were a bit older than other champion horses on the farm but they'd produced the most winners. "Can't Bree give the guy a tour?" Shoot, his sister was in charge of the horse barns.

"The buyer's name is Peter Westin. He's a former PRCA champion steer wrestler."

"I thought my rodeo career was a black mark on the family name," Riley teased.

His father wasn't in a humorous mood. "You have more in common with Westin than I do and I need your help closing the deal."

"I'm riding in every rodeo from here to who-knows-where the next two months."

"You can fly in for one night, can't you?"

"I don't know. Maybe."

"I backed off you because your mother asked me to. You've done what you've wanted most of your adult life. You hardly visit anymore."

Guilt trip. Riley hadn't been home in months. He missed Belle Farms but kept his distance because he didn't care to argue with his father. *Family money pays your entry fees.* "I'll be there."

"Good. Your mother's planning a formal dinner."

"Yeah, sure."

"How's the *Dark Stranger* flying?"

"Runs like a dream," Riley lied. No sense troubling

the old man when he hadn't learned the extent of the damages.

"Stay safe, son."

"Will do. 'Bye, Dad." Riley disconnected the call and shoved the phone into his back pocket. There were times that he wished he had his act together. His father's request to schmooze a potential horse buyer was an attempt to lure Riley back to Belle Farms and persuade him to give up rodeo.

Having unlimited funds at his disposal had allowed Riley to avoid making decisions about his future. He'd promised his father if he could bust broncs in college he'd earn a degree then return to the farm. Instead, after he'd graduated he'd decided to try his hand at professional rodeo—two years max. Riley was into his third season of the sport and his father was running out of patience.

Although he'd never admit it out loud, Riley didn't love rodeo as much as he pretended to, but the alternative—working with thoroughbred racing horses—was enough to keep him competing. Until he knew what he wanted to do with his life, he refused to quit the circuit. Not many twenty-five-year-olds had mapped out their lives but Riley feared even by Maria's age he wouldn't have a plan for his future.

Gear bag in hand, he moseyed into the stands to watch the rest of the rodeo. Later he'd grab a bite to eat then find a motel and call it a night. While other cowboys headed to the local watering hole, Riley would end the evening alone…dreaming about a woman more than three hundred miles away.

LATE SUNDAY AFTERNOON, MARIA pointed to the sky and said, "That's him." Riley Fitzgerald—the hot, young rodeo cowboy whose memory had disrupted her sleep the past two nights. She checked her watch. Four-thirty on the dot. Riley had phoned her before he'd left Payson and asked to meet her father at the airport.

The moment the plane's wheels touched down, Maria's heartbeat accelerated. Seeing Riley again wasn't a good idea, but that hadn't stopped her from accompanying her father this afternoon. The cowboy excited her and it had been longer than she remembered since a man had rattled her cage.

Too bad more than an age difference raised red flags in Maria's head. In the brief time she'd known Riley she'd sensed he lived life in the moment, thinking only of himself. That wasn't necessarily a bad thing—most young adults were self-centered. Those days had passed Maria by and now her mission in life was to put herself last and help others first.

Riley taxied toward the hangar.

"I'm surprised," her father said.

"About what?"

"That a young man his age is an accomplished pilot."

Landing a plane with winds gusting at thirty-five miles per hour wasn't easy but Riley managed the feat without mishap. Maria guessed that behind his cocky cowboy charm was a serious aviator.

"Twenty-five isn't that young," she said, drawing a frown from her father. When Maria had been Riley's age she'd already earned a master's degree and had begun work on her doctorate. She'd watched her brother die and had helped her parents plan the funeral.

"Your brother would have been twenty-five next month."

"I know." She'd never forget the night Juan had been

gunned down. Maria had arrived at the E.R. in time to hold her brother's hand and beg his forgiveness as he'd slipped away.

Less than a minute after Riley parked the plane, the cockpit door opened and he stepped into view. He wore aviator sunglasses but she knew the moment he spotted her—he flashed his devil-may-care grin.

"Nice to see you again, Mr. Alvarez." Riley removed his glasses and his eyes pinned her. "Hello, Maria."

Was it her imagination or had her name slid off his tongue in a husky whisper? "How was your flight?" The question squeaked past her lips.

"Good." Riley switched his attention to her father. "Did you have a chance to drive out to the salvage yard and check on the Cessna?"

"Sí." While her father discussed the list of recommended repairs with Riley, Maria wandered over to the soda machine. Maybe a Coke—make that a Diet Coke—would settle her nerves. She hated diet soda, and was disgusted with herself for caring about Riley's opinion of her figure. What did it matter if she needed to lose ten pounds? She and Riley weren't lovers. Shoot, they weren't friends, either. That Maria was even having this conversation with herself annoyed her.

Propping a shoulder against the wall, she studied Riley. He glanced her way and she swore the corner of his mouth curved in an intimate acknowledgment of her interest in him. Her pulse shifted into overdrive. Oh, who was she kidding? Riley was a cowboy. Flirting was in his DNA. If Maria were five years younger, she wouldn't be as self-conscious of her attraction to

Riley. She tossed the half-empty soda can into the re-
cycle bin then joined the men.

"How long until the repairs are completed?" Riley
asked.

"It will be ten days before the propeller parts come
in."

"I'll pay double your hourly wage to work on the
Dark Stranger."

Maria flinched. Ricardo Alvarez was a prideful
man. "I will fix it for—"

"Mr. Alvarez. You've already taken the time to
drive out to the salvage yard to inspect the plane."
Riley fished his wallet from his pocket and handed
her father a credit card. "Use this to cover moving the
plane, parts and supplies." He turned to Maria and
asked, "Will you join me for dinner?"

Oh, my God. He'd asked her out on a date in front
of her father? "Ah…"

"I didn't have a chance to celebrate my win this
weekend and I was hoping you'd share a victory meal
with me." Riley's gaze roamed over her and Maria felt
her face flame.

Even though her family never ate together anymore
she hoped her father would provide an excuse to decline the dinner invitation. "Did you or Mom have anything planned for supper?"

"No."

Thanks, Dad.

She made a feeble attempt to back out of the date.
"Aren't you flying to another rodeo?"

"I'm free until next weekend." He glanced at her
father. "I'll hang around Albuquerque this week in case
you need an extra pair of hands to work on the plane."

Doubting her father would appreciate Riley's help,

Maria said, "We'd better get going." She headed for her station wagon in the parking lot. *She* and not some young, wealthy, full-of-himself, sexy, hot rodeo cowboy would call the shots tonight.

Before she'd put the car in Reverse, Maria's cell phone rang.

"Bad news?" Riley asked after she ended the call.

"It's Cruz."

"What happened?" The note of concern in Riley's voice startled Maria.

"He was arrested."

"What'd he do?" Riley braced a hand against the dashboard as Maria sped from the airport.

"Defacing private property."

"Cruz joined the Los Locos?"

Riley remembered.

Maria ignored the pleasant feeling that rushed through her at the knowledge that Riley had listened to her ramblings about the Los Locos gang. Used to having her lectures go in one ear of her students' and out the other she'd assumed the same for Riley since he was closer in age to Cruz than her.

"I don't know if he was alone or with the gang." Maria's thoughts turned inward. Cruz's mother wouldn't be able to post bail and the school district's strict policy prohibiting teachers from posting bond for students prevented Maria from interceding on Cruz's behalf. What a mess. She pulled into the police station and parked in a visitor's stall. "Wait here."

"Are you kidding?" Riley trailed after her.

As soon as she stepped inside the precinct building an officer intercepted her. "Maria, we can't release him into your custody." Carlos Bradshaw had attended high school with Maria and did his best to help her students when they landed in jail.

Carlos glanced at Riley. "Who are you?"

"Riley Fitzgerald." He held out a hand.

Carlos's eyes narrowed as he examined Riley's attire.

"Riley's a rodeo cowboy," Maria said.

Carlos wasn't impressed. "Cruz has to post bail to get out. And if he doesn't appear at his hearing he'll do time in juvie."

"Cruz's mother doesn't have the money and you know I'll lose my job if I post his bail." Maria shuddered at the thought of Cruz spending the night in lock-up with drug addicts, pedophiles and gangbangers.

"How much is his bond?" Riley asked.

"Ten thousand," Carlos said.

"I'll cover it."

"You must be pretty good at rodeoing if you have that much money to spare," Carlos said.

"Last year's world champion in the saddle-bronc competition." Riley removed his checkbook from his shirt pocket.

"I'll tell them Cruz will make bail." Carlos stopped at the information desk and spoke to the clerk.

"Why are you doing this?" Maria asked.

"The kid needs help."

"You don't even know Cruz."

"I know you," Riley said. "And you care about what happens to Cruz."

Maria's heart melted. Maybe she'd misjudged Riley and there was more to the man than a pretty face, a sexy grin and a fat wallet.

Chapter Five

Riley stood in the police station foyer, a shoulder propped against the wall, waiting for Officer Bradshaw to retrieve Cruz from the holding cell. Maria had left to sign paperwork for the teenage delinquent.

"What are you doing here?" Cruz said when he spotted Riley.

"Bailing you out." Riley noted the teen's pale complexion. "First time in the joint?"

Cruz ignored the question and glared at Bradshaw, who had hold of his arm.

"Better be the last time." The officer released the teen. "Maria asked that you wait here for her." Bradshaw shoved Cruz toward the bench in the middle of the hall then lowered his voice. "What's your angle in all this?"

"How do mean?" Riley asked.

"Why'd you post bail for the kid? Trying to get on Maria's good side?"

"Maybe." To tell the truth, Riley wasn't sure if his attraction to Maria had prompted him to intervene or if there was more going on inside him than impressing the teacher.

"I don't know what your game is, but you aren't her type."

Because he was a few years younger or because he was wealthy? "Who is her type?"

Rather than answer, Bradshaw did an about-face and walked off. Riley moseyed over to the bench and sat next to Cruz. "Why'd you spray paint the building?"

The kid gaped at Riley as if he was nuts. "Ahh… cuz I wanted to?"

Riley didn't know the first thing about communicating with teenagers.

"You got any goals in life besides defacing property and causing general mayhem?"

"Why do you care what I do?"

"I don't. I'm curious."

"Doesn't matter what I do 'cause one day I'm gonna get clipped."

"Maria told me about your brother. I'm sorry, Cruz."

The kid shrugged off the condolence. Riley shuddered at the thought of waking each morning worried he'd be dead by suppertime.

"You ever visit your father in prison?" Riley asked.

"No."

"Your father was a heck of a bull rider. I didn't know him personally but his name comes up on the circuit every now and then."

The tidbit of information piqued Cruz's curiosity. "What do they say about him?"

"They claim T. C. Rivera was part bull himself." Riley grinned. "Your father could predict a bull's next move before the bull."

"I never saw him ride."

"You ever think about rodeoing?"

"Where am I gonna get a bull to practice on?"

"You're too lanky to ride bulls. You're built to bust broncs."

"Don't matter. There's no broncs in the 'hood."

An idea percolated in Riley's head. "If I could scare up a practice bronc would you want to try your hand at busting one?"

"Rodeo's stupid. That's why my dad's in the slammer."

Riley baited Cruz. "What's the matter? Afraid you might get hurt?"

"No." The kid glared. "Fallin' off a horse is easy compared to taking a bullet from a passing car."

"You've been shot?"

"Once." Cruz bunched his shirtsleeve, exposing a scar above his elbow. A quarter inch of flesh was missing.

"Bet that hurt."

"No shit."

"How old were you?"

"Nine."

Nine years old? No wonder kids in the 'hood held out little hope for a better life. They were marking time until their end came.

"You must make a lot of money at rodeo if you fly your own plane and wear those sissy boots." Cruz smirked.

"The better cowboys make decent money." If he confessed the cash in his wallet came from his trust fund and not rodeo wins or sponsorships, Cruz wouldn't bother with the sport. "If bullets don't scare you, then why not try—"

"Try what?" Maria appeared out of nowhere.

"Rodeo," Riley said. "Better hobby than drawing pictures on buildings."

"Cruz doesn't have time for hobbies. The judge has generously decided to give you a community-service sentence rather than make you stand trial for vandalism."

Maria must have done some fast-talking to change the judge's mind.

"What kind of community service?" Cruz asked.

"Garbage detail."

"No way." Cruz popped off the bench. "I ain't bagging no stinkin' trash."

"Then you sit in the waiting cell until your trial."

Riley admired Maria for playing hardball and not backing down to the kid.

"How long do I have to collect trash for?"

"A hundred hours," Maria said.

Cruz's mouth sagged open.

"The earliest the judge would hear your case is in seven weeks. You're welcome to wait in jail until then."

"What about my GED? Did you tell the judge about all the tests I have to take?"

"Yes, but the judge said if you'd cared about your education you would have been at home studying instead of tagging property with the Los Locos."

"She's a juvie judge. Doesn't she give a shit about kids?"

Maria shoved a hand through her hair. "Cruz, you've been offered a lot of second chances and you've done nothing with them. Nobody cares about you or your GED." She set her hand on his shoulder. "Except me."

He shrugged off her touch. "Man, this sucks!"

"Before you two decide anything, give me five minutes." Riley stepped outside the building and phoned Ed Parker. After a quick chat, he asked Ed for his father's cell number. Gil Parker answered on the first ring.

Riley asked the man if he'd allow a teenage juvenile offender to serve his community-service sentence at the Gateway Ranch. Without going into detail Riley explained Cruz's situation and how Maria was helping the teen and two of his buddies earn their GEDs. Gil agreed to take all three boys in for the rest of the summer as long as they worked for their room and board.

"New game plan," Riley said when he entered the building.

"Cruz's situation doesn't involve you," Maria said.

Riley raised his hand. "Hold up a second."

"Yeah, Ms. Alvarez," Cruz said. "Maybe Riley can get me off the hook."

"No can do, kid, but I've got a better idea for you than garbage detail."

"And what would that plan be?" Maria asked.

"First, I need to see the judge." Riley approached the station desk. "Is there any way I can have a word with the judge handling Cruz Rivera's case?" When the clerk eyed him suspiciously, he said, "Officer Bradshaw will vouch for me."

"One minute." The clerk disappeared through a door at the back of the room. A moment later she returned with Maria's cop friend.

"What's going on?" Bradshaw asked.

"Take me to the judge who ruled on Cruz's case," Riley said.

"Why?"

"There's a better way to teach Cruz to stay away from gangs than picking up trash."

"If you're wasting the judge's time, I'll toss you in a holding cell," Bradshaw warned.

After a series of twists and turns through several hallways they arrived at the judge's chamber. Bradshaw knocked twice.

"Enter," a feminine voice called.

"Judge Hamel." Bradshaw poked his head around the door. "Do you have a minute for a friend of Maria Alvarez?"

"Make it fast."

Riley followed Bradshaw into the room, which wasn't much bigger than his mother's master bedroom closet. What happened to judges having plush offices with designer furniture? This woman's desk was a gray metal monstrosity covered with dents and scratches. Instead of original paintings on the walls, a poster of the Eiffel Tower hung behind the desk and a cheap put-it-together-yourself bookcase leaned against the wall with sickly plants resting on the top shelf. The windowless cubicle smelled of coffee and peppermints.

"Sit down." The judge pointed her pen at the folding chair in front of the desk, then removed her reading glasses and tossed them onto the open file in front of her.

"Ma'am, my name is Riley Fitzgerald." He tipped his hat. The judge, who had to be in her sixties, eyeballed him from head-to-toe. He hoped his rodeo-cowboy charisma worked on the judge. "I have a suggestion for Cruz Rivera's sen—"

"Are you telling me how to do my job—" her eyes narrowed "—cowboy?"

"No, ma'am. But I'm hoping you'll be open to the idea of Cruz working off his service hours at a ranch."

Bradshaw chuckled, but Riley ignored the officer.

"What's a city boy going to do on a ranch, Mr. Fitzgerald?"

"Muck out horse stalls for a start, ma'am."

"Hmm…" The judge tapped her pen on the desk then asked, "Where's this ranch?"

"The Gateway Ranch north of Albuquerque. Gil Parker is the—"

"I know Gil. He serves on the city's environmental community board."

Even better.

The judge leaned back in her chair and assessed Riley. "You're a real cowboy, Mr. Fitzgerald?"

Riley poured on the charm. "I'm a rodeo cowboy, ma'am."

"It's 'Your Honor.'"

"Yes, ma'am, Your Honor. I'm the reigning PRCA world saddle-bronc champion."

"I have no idea what that means." She waved a hand in the air. "Nor do I care. Now tell me why you're interested in helping Cruz Rivera?"

Mostly Riley wanted to intervene for Maria's sake. "Maria's working hard to help Cruz earn his GED and she really cares about the kid succeeding." Cruz staying at the Gateway Ranch would give Riley an excuse to keep in touch with Maria. "If Cruz lives and works at the ranch, Maria can focus her energy on tutoring him and not trying to keep him out of trouble."

The judge remained silent.

"Cruz's father was a bull rider—"

"I'm aware of the young man's family history."

"Ranch chores are tough—more difficult than trash detail. Living at the ranch would keep Cruz off the streets and away from gangs. Plus, he'd have to learn to take orders from the other cowboys."

After a long silence the judge lifted her gavel and slammed it against the wood block resting on the corner of the desk. Riley's ears rang. "I'll change his sentence to the Gateway Ranch." She glanced at Bradshaw. "Send Maria back in here." She narrowed her eyes. "Your plan had better work, Mr. Fitzgerald. If I receive one complaint about Cruz from Gil Parker or anyone else at the Gateway Ranch, I'll ship Cruz off to juvie."

"Thank you, ma'—I mean, Your Honor. You won't regret this."

"See that I don't, cowboy."

Bradshaw escorted Riley to the main corridor of the police station.

"Where did you go?" Maria asked.

"To see the judge," Riley said.

"Judge Hamel wants you in her chambers, Maria," Bradshaw said.

"What's going on, Riley?" Maria asked.

"The judge agreed to allow Cruz to work off his community-service hours doing ranch work."

"What ranch?" Maria asked.

"Gateway Ranch—north of the city."

"What do I gotta do?" Cruz frowned.

"Muck out horse stalls," Riley said.

"Huh?" Cruz turned to Maria for clarification.

"Scoop horse poop."

"After Cruz finishes his chores," Riley said, "I'll show him the rodeo ropes."

"You're staying at the Gateway Ranch?" Maria asked.

Riley shrugged. "The foreman of the ranch is the father of a rodeo buddy of mine."

"I won't be able to drive Cruz out to the ranch every day."

"There's a bunkhouse on the property. Cruz can stay there."

Maria folded her arms across her chest, the action raising her breasts higher. Riley did his best to ignore the twinge in his groin. "What about his schoolwork?" she asked.

"What about my homies?" Cruz added.

"Gil invited Victor and Alonso to tag along with Cruz as long as all three work for their room and board."

"I don't get paid?" Cruz protested.

"Nope," Riley said.

"Once I do my hundred hours, I ain't sticking around no ranch."

"With all three guys at the ranch—" Riley spoke to Maria "—you'd only have to make a few trips a week out there to tutor them."

"I can manage that, but I'll have to clear the arrangement with their families."

"So that's it?" Cruz glared. "You guys make all the decisions and I get no say?"

"You lost your *say* when you landed in jail," Maria said.

"Man, this blows."

Maria dug through her purse and handed a set of keys to the teen. "Wait in my car." Once he left the building, Maria said, "I don't know how to thank you, Riley. We could use more mentors in our program."

Riley had never thought of himself as a mentor but the idea of helping Cruz and the other boys made him feel useful and for the first time unselfish. For once he was thinking of someone other than himself.

Maria stood on tiptoe and kissed his cheek. Caught off guard, he had no time to absorb the sensation of her lips brushing his skin, her sigh caressing his chin. "Thank you for caring."

Stunned, he watched Maria head to the judge's chambers. He hoped his plan to help the three delinquent amigos didn't backfire, because Riley intended to earn another kiss from Maria—next time on the mouth.

"YOU SUCK, CRUZ," VICTOR said in the backseat of Maria's station wagon. "Because of you I gotta go to a stupid ranch and shovel horse turds."

Maria clenched the steering wheel as she felt a wave of heartburn coming on. Victor and Alonso weren't thrilled about keeping Cruz company while he worked off his community-service hours. Their attitude didn't surprise her. The three seventeen-year-olds had never held down real jobs. Local businesses were reluctant to hire them because of their juvenile records and suspensions from school. She didn't envy the cowboy put in charge of supervising the boys.

Gaining approval from the teens' parents had been easier than Maria had anticipated. Once she'd assured them that their sons would continue working toward their GEDs the parents had conceded it was in their sons' best interest to be removed from the influence of the Los Locos gang.

"I didn't force you to come," Cruz said. "Blame it on Ms. Alvarez's boyfriend."

Boyfriend? "Mr. Fitzgerald is not my boyfriend. He's trying to help you, Cruz."

"He wants to get in your—" The rest of Cruz's

remark came out in a grunt after Alonso elbowed him in the chest.

Maria slowed the car, then turned off the road and drove beneath a huge arch with the name Gateway Ranch burned into the wood. Three days had passed since Riley had returned from the rodeo in Arizona. Maria had dropped him off at the hotel Sunday night after they'd posted Cruz's bail. She waited until late Monday afternoon to call him to see if he'd wanted to eat dinner with her. The hotel clerk informed her that he'd already checked out of his room. That Riley hadn't told her his plans shouldn't have mattered—they weren't a couple. But he'd offered to help her students and...

And what? That gives you a right to know his every move?

Finally, on Tuesday, Riley had phoned her and said he'd rented a pickup and was staying at the Gateway Ranch getting things ready for the boys. He'd told her to bring the teens out Wednesday and he'd help supervise them until Friday morning when he flew to a rodeo in Nevada.

"There's a lot of stinkin' cows on this place," Victor said as they drove along the gravel road.

Maria glanced at the grazing herd. She'd done a little research on the ranch and decided to share her findings with the boys. "The Gateway Ranch runs over ten thousand head of cattle. Robert Masterson purchased the property back in 1812."

"Guess he's dead now." Cruz snickered.

"Masterson never married. When he died, he left the ranch to a widowed schoolteacher in town."

"What'd she do with the place?" Alonso asked.

"Sold it to the bank. The bank split the property into three parcels then sold off two and kept the third."

"So the Gateway is one of those parcels?" Victor asked.

"Yes." Maria was glad the boys appeared interested in the area's history. "Francis Wellington bought one parcel and a man named Buck Honorable bought the other. As the story goes, Buck and Francis did not get along and fought over water rights and property lines. They even accused each other of cattle rustling."

"What's that?" Victor asked.

"Stealing cows," Alonso answered.

"The fighting got so bad," Maria continued, "that Buck challenged Francis to a duel."

"Who won?" Cruz asked.

Maria didn't answer right away as she maneuvered the car around an outcropping of rock. Once she negotiated the tight turn, she stopped the vehicle and shifted into Park. "Wow."

Thousands of milling cows dotted the green valley below. A collection of barns, corrals, holding pens and various ranch buildings were scattered about.

"This place is huge." Victor pressed his face against the window.

"To answer your question, Cruz, Francis won the duel, because Buck's rifle accidentally discharged and he shot himself in the chest."

"What an idiot," Cruz said.

"Hey, Ms. Alvarez." Victor tapped her shoulder. "You think we're gonna get our own horse to ride while we're here?"

"I don't know. I'm sure one of the ranch hands would teach you to ride."

Victor nudged Alonso. "You wanna learn how to ride a horse?"

"Yeah, sure."

Maria put the car into Drive. "First we need to introduce ourselves to Mr. Parker. He's in charge of the day-to-day operation of the ranch. In other words, all of you had better do as he says."

"Nobody bosses me around," Cruz said.

Maria had had enough of the teen's obstinate attitude. "Say the word, Cruz, and I'll take you back to the police station, where you can wait until your trial."

Seconds passed.

"Whatever. I don't give a crap," Cruz said.

Tense silence filled the car as Maria pulled into the ranch yard. "There's Riley!" Victor pointed out the windshield.

Alonso leaned over the front seat to see out the window. "Where?"

"In the corral."

Riley sat astride a bucking gelding—every inch the quintessential cowboy. He gripped a rope in his right hand, his left arm raised high above his head as he spurred the horse along its neck.

Ranch hands gathered near the pen, straddling the top rail or poking their heads through the slats for a better view. Maria lowered her window and excited shouts filtered into the car.

"Check it out, Cruz. The dude's a real pro." Alonso spared his friend a glance, but Cruz acted unimpressed, arms folded over his chest as if bored by the action in the corral.

Maria forgot about the boys as she watched Riley. His young, athletic body swayed and jerked in rhythm to the horse's bucking. Horse and rider melded into one, performing a ballet of wild gyrations and explosive movements. Seconds passed and the bucking grew weaker. Weaker. Finally the horse conceded defeat and came to a standstill, its sides heaving.

"That was totally cool!" Victor said.

"Anyone can do that if you hold on long enough," Cruz grumbled.

"Let's congratulate Riley." Maria stepped from the car and slammed the door. The noise spooked the gelding. The horse kicked his back legs out and Riley sailed over the animal's head.

Oh, dear. Twenty sets of eyes glared at Maria.

Riley got to his feet and dusted himself off. He retrieved his hat from across the pen then turned to see what had startled the bronc. An older man broke away from the pack and headed toward Maria. Lines etched his face and he walked with a pronounced limp.

"Gil Parker." He tipped his hat. "You must be the teacher Riley mentioned." The foreman didn't smile as he sized up the boys. Alonso and Victor dropped their gazes but Cruz stared defiantly at the older man. "You're the troublemaker." Mr. Parker spoke to Cruz.

Cruz's chin jutted but he remained tightlipped. A short, gray-haired man with a scruffy beard joined the group. He turned his head to the side and spit tobacco juice twenty feet through the air.

"Aw, dude, that was insane," Victor said.

"What'd ya call me, son?" The old man squinted, his eyes disappearing in the wrinkled folds of skin.

"Sir. I meant, sir," Victor stammered. "Can you teach me how to spit?"

"Depends."

"On what?" Victor asked.

"On how well ya follow orders."

"Hey," Riley called out. He stopped at Maria's side. "Let me introduce everyone." Riley put a hand on each boy's shoulder as he said their name. "Cruz, Alonso and Victor." He moved his hand to Maria's shoulder and her skin warmed beneath his touch. "Maria Alvarez. She's helping the boys earn their GEDs."

Riley motioned to the cowboys. "This is Gil Parker, he runs the place. His son and I compete at many of the same rodeos throughout the year." Riley pointed to the old man. "This here is Shorty. He's worked at the Gateway Ranch for over twenty years."

"How old are you?" Alonso asked.

"Old 'nough to give Jesus a run fer his money."

"Shorty works with the ranch horses," Mr. Parker said. "You boys will report to Shorty and take your orders from him."

"Ya youngins gotta be outfitted proper if yer gonna do cowboy work," Shorty said.

"What's the matter with my clothes?" Cruz tugged on his baggy pants.

"Nothin' less'n ya wanna make a spectacle a yerself." He eyed the teen's outfit. "Looks like ya done dropped a load in yer undershorts."

Cruz's face reddened.

"We'll take good care of your students, Ms. Alvarez." Gil Parker tipped his hat and left the group.

"I'll show ya where yer gonna bunk down." Shorty walked off and the boys followed.

"They'll be fine," Riley said.

"I hope so." Maria wanted this arrangement to work out for the boys; but Shorty was so…short and old that she worried the teens would overwhelm the coot.

"Shorty's been a wrangler all his life and he used to ride bulls in his younger days. Handling three delinquent teens will be a breeze. You wait and see. The boys won't get away with anything under his watch."

Riley grasped Maria's hand. "How about a tour of the ranch?" Riley tugged her after him, his fingers tightening around hers.

He talked about the chores the boys would be doing but Maria didn't hear a word. She was too busy enjoying the warmth of Riley's callused fingers clasping hers.

Chapter Six

"Ya missed a turd."

Riley poked his head inside the barn and caught Shorty pointing the end of a pitchfork into a horse stall. Cruz towered over the old man by several inches.

"One turd isn't gonna make a difference." Despite his protest, Cruz snatched the rake from Shorty and flung the clump of soiled hay into a nearby wheelbarrow. "Satisfied?"

Wincing at the teen's rudeness, Riley hid in the shadows and eavesdropped. Shorty's head wasn't visible but Riley had a clear view of Cruz above the stall door.

"Ain't gonna be satisfied 'til ya do the job right, 'n' that means gittin' rid a the dirty straw."

"Why? The horse is gonna pee and crap all over the new hay."

"That's what horses do best, son. Pee 'n' drop turds."

"Being a cowboy sucks."

"I disagree, son. I'm partial to the cowboy way."

"Quit calling me 'son.'"

"Where'd ya git that chip on yer shoulder?"

"If you lived in my neighborhood, you'd act tough to survive, too."

Shorty moved into view and leaned against the grooming post in the center aisle. He dug out a tobacco pouch from his shirt pocket and stuffed a pinch of chew between his cheek and gum. "If ya don't care fer livin' there, git out."

"It's not that easy to leave." Cruz stepped from the stall.

"All ya gotta do is pack yer bags 'n' vamoose."

"And go where? What would I do?"

Cruz's questions reminded Riley of the privileged life he led. He'd never had to worry about clothes, food, or shelter—all taken for granted. Gangs provided kids in the 'hood with the same securities. The rabble-rousers made easy money dealing drugs, robbing stores, pickpocketing people and selling stolen property. The money they amassed offered its members a lifestyle they'd only dreamed of—cars, expensive clothes, shoes, guns, liquor and all the food they could eat. Aside from escaping poverty, being a gangbanger fed their self-esteem—the kids became big shots.

"Git a job fer starters." Shorty spit tobacco at the drain in the barn floor.

"Nice shot." Cruz set the pitchfork aside and wiped his brow—probably the first time the kid had perspired from honest hard work. "Even if I get my GED who's gonna hire me? I got a juvie record."

"Sellin' drugs?"

"No, but that's where the big money is." Cruz pitched another forkful of soiled hay into the wheelbarrow. "I had a joint in my pocket when the cops nailed me for shoplifting. I was keeping it for a friend."

Shorty snickered at the kid's outright lie.

"Whatever, man."

"The boss said yer doin' community service at the ranch. What'd they catch ya for?"

"Tagged an office building with my homies. The judge gave me trash detail but my teacher's boyfriend convinced her I'd learn my lesson better shoveling horseshit, so I got sent here."

"Ya any good at drawin'?"

"Do you ask this many questions all the time?"

"Ain't got nothin' better to do while I watch ya work." Shorty ignored the cuss word that slipped from Cruz's mouth. "Ya ever see yer father?"

"You know my old man?"

"T. C. Rivera was a dang good bull rider 'fore he landed in jail."

"He killed a man in self-defense, but the stupid lawyers—"

"Lawyers ain't ignorant, son."

"Then the jury hated Latinos, because my dad got the maximum sentence. If he would have been white he'd have been charged with manslaughter and been out of prison by now."

"Yer dad got what he deserved. I was there. I saw everythin'."

Riley hadn't known Shorty had witnessed the infamous brawl at Deadwood Dick's Gaming Hall in Deadwood, South Dakota, three weeks prior to the finals in Las Vegas.

"Wanna hear the truth or keep believin' the rumors?"

"The truth." Cruz rested the pitchfork against the stall door and sat on a bale.

"I rode bulls in my heyday, kid. Rode 'til I broke most every bone in my body. When I couldn't ride no more, I started clownin' in rodeos. I was at the bar the night T.C. pulled a knife on Clarence Hinkley."

"My father defended himself."

"He tell ya that?"

Cruz shook his head.

"T.C. was drunk. He couldn't hold his liquor—lotta cowboys can't. By the time Clarence walked into the gamin' hall T.C. was a swayin' and stumblin'."

"The other guy should have known better than to harass my dad."

"Cowboys talk a good game, son. Part a bein' a cowboy. Clarence taunted T.C. 'bout his ride that day."

"What'd he say?"

"Said yer father's luck had run out 'n' he ought to use his pretty face fer ridin' women not bulls." Shorty paused to spit.

"If that's all the guy said, why'd my father kill him?"

"Don't believe T.C. meant to. Think he wanted to scare Clarence when he pulled a knife."

"How come no one stopped my dad?"

"I tried."

"You?"

Shorty yanked the snaps apart on the front of his western shirt. Even from his hiding place at the end of the barn, Riley saw the jagged scar that dissected the ranch hand's chest.

"T.C. slashed me when I stepped in front a him."

Cruz's mouth dropped open. "My father did that to you?"

"Other cowboys got nicked, too, 'cause they tried to stop T.C. The barkeep stuck his boot out 'n' tripped yer father. T.C. fell forward and Clarence didn't have time to git outta the way. The knife went straight through his heart. Died right there on the floor."

"It was an accident, then."

"Partly. But at the end a the night a man was dead and yer father was holdin' the knife."

"He was drunk. He didn't know what he was doing."

"There comes a time when a man has to own up to his actions. T.C. might not a meant to kill Clarence, but he did."

"Where do you want me to dump this crap anyway?" Cruz kicked the wheelbarrow.

"Compost pile's out back o' the barn."

Cruz pushed the barrow past Riley and out the barn doors.

"Ya can quit hidin' 'n' come out now."

"Hey, Shorty. How's Cruz doing?"

"His mouth works good—full of wind as a hoss with colic."

"I didn't know you hung around the circuit after you retired."

Shorty waved off Riley's comment. "'Nough talk 'bout me. Hear yer havin' trouble stickin' to the saddle this season."

The very reason Riley had returned to the Gateway Ranch this morning. He'd ushered in the beginning of September with a loss during the first go-round in the Nevada rodeo. "Can't seem to win the big ones."

"Ya got a buckle already. Ain't one enough?"

Riley scoffed. "I didn't *earn* that buckle."

"Well, then, shouldn't ya be practicin' 'stead a hangin' 'round here babysittin' delinquents?"

"I promised Maria I'd make sure the boys settled in at the ranch." He checked his watch. "She should arrive within the hour."

"Ain't surprised a woman's the reason ya——"

"What are you doing here?" Cruz stepped inside the barn, his glare directed at Riley.

"Got a stubborn horse that needs the wild ridden out of him. You interested?" When Cruz didn't respond, Riley said, "Once I work the kinks out of him, you can take a stab at staying in the saddle."

"Am I done with chores?" Cruz asked Shorty.

"After ya fill the grain buckets yer done."

"Meet me at the corral," Riley said.

"Yeah, whatever." Cruz disappeared into the storage room.

"What happens if ya don't win this year?" Shorty asked.

"Not sure." That was the God's honest truth. Riley left the barn, his purposeful strides eating the ground as he headed to the round pen.

WHAT IN THE WORLD?

Maria parked the station wagon in front of the main house at the Gateway Ranch and watched the crowd gathered near the livestock pen. Unable to see over the heads of the cowboys, she left the car and zigzagged between the trucks parked helter-skelter in the ranch yard.

"Excuse me. Pardon me." Maria pushed her way through the throng of smelly cowboys until she had a clear view of the commotion inside the pen—Cruz sitting atop a bucking horse. She hardly recognized the teen in slim-fitting Wranglers, work boots and a navy blue T-shirt. Used to seeing him in baggy clothes, Cruz was skinnier than she'd realized.

Right then the horse kicked its back legs out and Cruz pitched forward in the saddle. Maria crossed her fingers, praying he wouldn't land on his face in the dirt.

"Hey, Ms. Alvarez!" Eyes bright with excitement, Victor squeezed past a ranch hand. "Cruz is bustin' a bronc."

"He sure is." She assessed Victor's outfit. The fitted clothes showed he could stand to lose a few pounds. "Nice duds."

"They suck, but I don't care as long as my homies in the 'hood don't see me."

Maria watched Cruz. The horse appeared to be tiring. "How many times has he done this?" She worried Cruz would get injured and be unable to complete his community-service sentence.

"Riley rides the buck out of the bronc first then Cruz finishes him off," Victor said.

Riley was here? She thought he'd left yesterday for a rodeo. Keeping track of everyone's schedules was a losing battle.

"You shoulda seen Riley when he rode the horse the first time. He got thrown twice."

Ouch. "Where's Alonso?"

"In the barn with the vet checking on a sick cow."

The horse in the corral finally settled down and the cowboys whistled and clapped. Cruz jumped off, a huge smile wreathing his face.

Maria hadn't seen the teen smile—a genuine smile—since she'd begun working with him. It was too early to tell if Riley's suggestion to leave the boys at the Gateway Ranch had been a good idea or not, but Cruz's improved demeanor gave her hope.

"Did you guys finish your school lessons?" she asked.

"We don't have time to study 'cause of all the work they make us do," Victor said.

"Shorty asks you to do chores late at night?"

"No—" Victor's face brightened "—but you should hear the stories the cowboys tell. Big Jim's great-great-grandfather was captured by the Sioux and they cut off one of his ears."

"This is a surprise." Riley's deep voice interrupted.

Amused by Victor's excited chatter, Maria hadn't realized the ranch hands had dispersed, leaving Riley and Cruz standing a few feet away inside the corral.

"Did you see me ride, Ms. Alvarez?"

"I sure did. That was a great performance. I'm impressed."

"Cruz has the raw talent to compete in this sport." Riley patted the teen's shoulder then spoke to Victor. "You want a turn on the horse?"

"Maybe next time. Big Jim wants me to help him fix the baler."

Victor spun but Maria grabbed his arm. "Wait. It's Saturday."

"So?"

"I drove out here to go over your school lessons. I don't want you falling behind." Two loud groans followed her announcement.

"I've got an idea," Riley said. "I'll take Ms. Alvarez on a horseback ride while you guys finish your chores."

Horseback ride? Maria had never ridden a horse on a merry-go-round, never mind a real one.

"When we return," Riley continued, "you have to crack open the books." He faced Maria. "How does that sound?"

"Wonderful." A horseback ride on a beautiful day

with a sexy, young cowboy—every thirtysomething woman's dream.

The teens high-fived and walked off toward the barn.

"What happened to the rodeo in Nevada?" Maria decided the beard stubble covering Riley's cheeks made him appear edgier...sexier—if that was possible.

"I lost the first go-round last night, so I returned early this morning."

Maria fought a smile. "I thought you were good at bustin' broncs."

"Full of sass today, eh?" Riley's eyes roamed over her body. "Glad you wore jeans."

"I should warn you that I've never ridden a horse."

"No problem. We'll ride double. Wait here."

Double. The word made her break out in a sweat. By the time Riley led a beautiful white mare from the barn, Maria was a nervous wreck. "This is Zelda. She's a trail horse—sturdy and sure-footed." Riley held out a straw cowboy hat. "To protect your face from the sun."

"Thanks." She plopped the hat on her head.

After lengthening the stirrups, Riley mounted then backed the horse against the corral rails. "Climb on behind me."

Maria eyed Riley's muscular buttocks and thighs. "There's not enough room for two in the saddle."

"Yes, there is. You'll see."

She climbed the rails then swung a leg over the back of Zelda. Riley scooted forward—less than an inch— and Maria wedged herself into the remaining space. Pelvis snugged against Riley's backside, her hormones skyrocketed off the charts.

"Wrap your arms around my waist and hang on." Riley clicked his tongue and urged Zelda into a trot.

Maria clung to Riley, not caring that her breasts were smashed against his back—the ground was a long way down.

"A quarter mile from here there's a trail that leads to a retention pond with a great view of the mountains," Riley said.

A quarter mile of sensual torture as her breasts absorbed the heat radiating off Riley's back. Forcing her lusty thoughts aside, Maria focused on the scenery, though her concentration was sorely tested by Riley's scent—faded cologne and earthy cowboy.

They rode in silence then turned south and followed a path behind an outcropping of rock. Maria noticed the retaining pond in the distance. Large piñon trees dotted the area, providing mottled shade. Riley reined in Zelda at the edge of the pond and helped Maria to the ground, then tied the horse's reins to a low hanging tree branch. Maria wasn't much of an outdoorsy person but the beauty before her was stunning.

Riley returned to her side and offered her a water bottle. He must have packed the drinks in the saddle pouch before he'd left the barn. "Let's rest in the shade," he said.

Maria checked for creepy-crawlies on the ground before sitting. Riley stretched out next to her—closer than was proper for *friends*. Maria was awed by Riley's masculinity. His muscular frame made her feel feminine and petite. He smiled as if he didn't have a care in the world.

"I envy you," she said.

"Why?"

"I might be wrong but I bet you view the bright side of things first." She shrugged. "I see the bad side. You wake in the morning eager to discover what the day holds in store for you. I roll out of bed and brace myself for what's to come."

"Life is too short to be miserable all the time," he said.

"You're only twenty-five." Maria laughed. "You haven't lived long enough for that saying to mean anything to you."

"Were you always this serious or did something happen to sober your outlook on life?"

The question caught Maria by surprise. Did she dare dredge up the past? The past was one of the reasons she needed to keep her defenses in place around Riley.

"You don't have to talk about it." Riley grasped her hand. "We can enjoy the quiet."

She liked that Riley didn't push her. His demeanor coaxed her to open up to him. "My brother was killed in a gang shooting ten years ago. He died at the age of fifteen."

The fingers around her hand tightened and Maria appreciated Riley's sympathy. "My brother came as a surprise to my parents. They thought they couldn't have any more children after me. I was ten years old when Juan was born and excited at playing the role of a big sister. We all doted on Juan. He could do no wrong in my parents' eyes."

Memories threatened to suffocate Maria. No matter how many years passed since her brother's death, the incident was never easy to talk about. "Juan began running with a wild bunch in his early teens. I was working on my doctorate degree and beginning my teaching career. I wasn't around enough to notice that his friends were members of a gang."

Maria paused, but Riley remained silent—add good listener to his list of admirable traits. "When

Juan didn't come home for three days straight my parents phoned me. I tracked my brother down. He'd been hanging out in an abandoned building with gang-bangers. Drinking. Smoking pot."

The stench of sewage and rotting garbage. Urine-stained mattresses had been thrown on the floor. Fast-food bags littered the stairwells. Rats scurried through the hallways. The hellhole remained vivid in Maria's mind.

"Juan begged me to give him a chance to leave the gang on his own before I told our parents." She swallowed hard. "I caved in and kept my mouth shut. Three days later Juan was gunned down two blocks from our home."

After all these years, the memory of that day was powerful enough to bring tears to her eyes. "No one came to his aid. Juan laid on the sidewalk for a half hour before the paramedics arrived. There were no witnesses—at least none that were brave enough to step forward. My brother remains another unsolved murder statistic."

"I'm sorry." Riley slipped his arm around Maria's shoulders and hugged her to his side.

"My parents were devastated. They couldn't understand why I didn't tell them as soon as I'd learned Juan had joined a gang. They never said as much but I saw it in their eyes—they blamed me for my brother's death." And rightly so. Maria had been twenty-five—an adult. She should have known better than to trust a fifteen-year-old to keep his word.

"Mom began drinking after the funeral. Dad shut down emotionally and immersed himself in his job, working overtime at the airport. Their hatred for delinquent teens has grown stronger through the years."

"Is that why you became involved in helping at-risk kids?"

"I believed if my parents could see that not all delinquent teens were bad seeds, they'd move on after my brother's death." And Maria had secretly hoped if her parents were able to put Juan's death behind them, that they'd forgive her for not giving them a chance to save their son.

"I bet your folks are proud of you," Riley said.

"They say I'm wasting my time on the kids."

"For what it's worth, I think what you do is incredible." He looked her in the eye. "I envy you having a purpose in life and being able to go after it in a meaningful way. You're making a difference in these kids' lives."

That was the nicest thing anyone had ever said to her. "Rodeo isn't your passion?"

"Bustin' broncs is a temporary gig. Down the road I want to—" He shrugged. "I don't know what I want to do."

"You have a college degree. Why not put that to use?"

"Maybe one day I will. Right now I can't picture myself sitting in an office eight-to-five. I enjoy the outdoors and I like having space around me."

Riley was a handsome, caring man, who'd offered to help a troubled teen when most people would have turned their backs. "Ever considered a career in social work?"

"Can't say I have."

"You'd be good at it."

"I think I'd be good at this." He leaned forward and brushed his lips over hers. The first touch of his mouth sent a jolt through Maria. When he slid his fingers across her cheek and deepened the kiss, she closed her eyes and gave herself over to the moment.

Riley wooed her with his tongue then gradually ended the kiss with little nibbles on her lip and soft pecks on her cheek. "Mmm. You taste good," he whispered. "Let's do that again."

"Keep your guns holstered, cowboy." A second kiss was a very bad idea.

"Why?"

Because you make me want you and I don't trust myself to stop us from going where we have no business going.

His eyes narrowed. "You think I'm too young for you, don't you?"

"As much as I enjoy your company and appreciate what you're doing for the boys, we're…well, we're wrong for each other on a lot of levels."

He stood and held out his hand. Once he helped her off the ground, he said, "I might be ten years younger, but in time I'll prove that I'm plenty man enough for you."

Riley got in the last word, because Maria was speechless.

Chapter Seven

Riley slowed Zelda to a walk as the mare drew near the ranch yard. He squelched the surge of frustration rising inside him. He'd have sold his best bucking saddle for another hour in the shade with Maria. But duty called and Maria was nothing if not dedicated to her charges. He closed his eyes and savored the heat of her lush breasts pressing against his back.

Kissing Maria had surpassed his wildest dreams. He'd expected her mouth to be memorable, but he hadn't been ready for the electrical charge that had hummed between them.

Aside from sexual compatibility, Riley and the teacher had one important trait in common—neither of them backed down from a challenge. Riley was determined to win a second world title and Maria intended for her three students to earn their GEDs. Riley's goal was physical, each step toward it lasting only eight seconds. Bustin' broncs carried risks, but so did Maria's job. Her goal consumed her entire day and most weekends, leaving no room in her schedule for relaxation and fun. Riley couldn't recall ever hearing her laugh—a deep, belly laugh that brought tears to her eyes.

Maria's life doesn't offer much to laugh about, idiot.

Riley admired her resolve to help delinquent teens and he sympathized with her struggle to come to terms with the role she'd played in her brother's death. He wished with all his heart he could tell her it hadn't been her fault, but the truth... If he'd been in her shoes and Bree had fallen in with the wrong crowd, he'd have felt the same sorrow and pain if he'd ignored the situation and as a result his sister had died.

Plenty of good people in the world suffered—life wasn't fair. Riley couldn't erase the past from Maria's memory, but maybe he could give her new memories to focus on. He guided Zelda to the horse trough then hopped off.

Maria made a move to get down, but Riley set his hand on her leg. "Wait until Zelda finishes drinking." Maria's brow glistened with perspiration and the front of her shirt sported two large damp spots. "You're hot."

"Riley..."

"Sweaty hot." He slid his hand along her thigh and she swallowed a moan.

"Zelda's done," Maria whispered.

He lifted his arms, offering to assist her to the ground.

"I can manage." Ignoring his help Maria shifted in the saddle, presenting him with a bird's-eye view of her fanny.

"A cowboy never allows a lady to dismount by herself." He clamped his hands on either side of her waist and set her on the ground. Taking Maria by the hand, Riley led the horse to the barn, where a ranch hand took the reins from him and escorted Zelda inside.

As they passed an eighteen-by-twenty-foot water-storage tank that stood four feet high, Maria said, "That's one huge horse trough."

"The ranch has a solar-powered well system," Riley explained. "Underground water is pumped to the surface and stored in this tank, then a network of pipes transports water to the horse troughs, the barn and the bunkhouse."

"The water's crystal clear."

Without thinking of the consequences Riley swung Maria into his arms, walked over to the tank and tossed her in. Her blood-curdling scream abruptly ended when she hit the water. The splash from her body soaked the front of Riley's shirt.

When Maria's head popped above the water's surface, she sputtered and gasped for air. "You...you..." She peeled her wet hair away from her eyes and glared.

Chuckling, he said, "You're mighty cute when you're angry."

She cupped her hands and hit the surface of the water, spewing a tidal wave at Riley. Drenched, he chuckled and joined the water fight, leaning over the edge of the tank. His hand accidently bumped her breast and the feel of the soft mound distracted him enough to drop his guard.

Maria wrapped an arm around his neck and tugged. Riley leaned closer ready to claim his reward. Right before their lips touched, Maria's fingers snaked through his belt loops. He lost his balance and tumbled over the side of the trough headfirst, boots pointed toward Heaven.

When he bobbed to the surface Maria stood on the opposite side of the tank laughing. Soaked to the bone she was the most beautiful woman he'd ever laid eyes on. He waded toward her, stopping only when his chest bumped hers.

"Riley, don't you dare—"

His mouth closed over hers and she melted into him. Man, she was good for his ego.

"What are you guys doing?"

Riley broke off their kiss and glanced over his shoulder. Victor, Cruz and Alonso stood outside the tank gaping at them.

"Follow my lead," Riley whispered in Maria's ear. They waded toward the boys then stopped. "On the count of three," Riley said. "One...two...three!"

In a synchronized movement, he and Maria swung their hands below the water surface and sent a huge wave over the edge. The boys yelped and stumbled backward, brushing at their soaked clothes.

"They peed their pants," Riley teased.

"Ah, man!" Cruz yelled.

"I'm coming in!" Victor charged the tank then vaulted into the air. Riley caught the teen around the waist, held him suspended over his head for a moment then released him. Victor hit the water with a smack but bobbed to the surface laughing.

"My turn!" Alonso retreated several feet before making a run for the tank. Maria scrambled out of the way and Riley braced himself when the teen launched into the air. Riley managed to hang on to Alonso long enough to twirl him around once before letting him go.

"Get in, Cruz!" Victor yelled.

Indecision showed on the teen's face. Right then Maria snuck behind Alonso and dunked him below the water.

"C'mon, Cruz. Join the fun!" Maria splashed him.

Riley held Maria prisoner around the waist. "Yeah,

Cruz, come dunk your teacher." He kissed Maria right before he pushed her head below the water. When Maria surfaced, Victor and Alonso pounced on her but this time she dragged the boys under with her.

"Watch out, I'm coming in!" Cruz dove over the edge.

"Get Riley!" Alonso led the charge. The boys closed in on Riley and Alonso jumped on his back. Victor grabbed him around the waist and Cruz dove under the water and went for his legs.

"Help, Maria!" Riley pleaded.

"No way. You started this." Maria scrambled toward the edge of the tank but her short legs and constant laughter made climbing to freedom impossible. "Somebody rescue me!"

Shorty appeared with a stepping stool and offered a helping hand. Instead of getting out of the tank Maria tugged Shorty in. The cowboy's hat went flying as he crashed into the water. When his bald head bobbed above the surface, the boys ganged up on him. Together, they managed to lift Shorty above their heads and spin him in a circle.

By now, a crowd had gathered. Maria managed to climb out of the tank and Riley followed.

"Who would have thought a water fight in a holding tank would be so much fun," Maria said.

When Riley noticed a ranch hand gawking at her wet clothes, he offered his soggy shirt as additional cover. She pressed the material to her breasts and giggled.

"What's so funny?" he asked.

"Your nipples are puckering, too," she said.

He leaned in and whispered, "My nipples aren't the only thing that's hard."

The quiet hitch in Maria's breath aroused Riley almost as much as the memory of kissing her.

Gil Parker stopped next to Riley and watched the commotion. "'Bout time someone cut Shorty down to size."

"I'll make sure the boys finish their chores before Maria tutors them," Riley said.

"We're throwing steaks and ribs on the barbecue." Gil glanced at Maria. "Be honored if you joined us for supper."

"Thank you, Mr. Parker. I'm afraid I didn't bring a change of clothes." She scowled at Riley. "I wasn't expecting to go for a swim."

"You're welcome to shower and change at the main house. Harriet will toss your clothes into the washer." Gil tipped his hat then walked off.

"Stay." Riley didn't want the day to end.

"I'll hang around for the cookout on one condition," Maria said.

"What's that?"

"You keep your hands to yourself…in and out of water tanks."

Riley raised his arms in the air. "Promise to keep my hands to myself."

But not my mouth.

MARIA SHOWERED IN THE GUEST bedroom bath while Gil Parker's housekeeper washed her clothes. As warm water cascaded over her shoulders her thoughts shifted to Riley.

The bronc rider had done what no other man had in a very long time—he'd made her laugh. She hadn't had this much fun in weeks…months…since before her split with Fernando. Being with Riley made her feel carefree, desirable and young at heart when most days she felt battered and battle-weary.

Have a fling with him. He's a cowboy. Cowboys do flings. They're not into long-term relationships.

Eyes closed, Maria envisioned Riley's naked, muscular chest. Her pulse pounded when she imagined his callused hands caressing her breasts, thighs... She hadn't had many lovers in her lifetime and she fantasized that Riley was as wild in bed as the broncs he rode.

Her body desired a man—not any man. She wanted Riley. Why couldn't she enjoy the here and now and live in the moment with him? Let whatever happens happen—until he moved on and out of her life for good? A fling sounded sensible but Riley had stolen a little piece of her heart when he'd gone out on a limb for the boys and secured a place for them at the Gateway Ranch.

The boys griped and complained about chores, but she sensed they were learning the value of hard work and that there was more to life than guns, gangs and violence. Even Cruz showed less of his tough-guy attitude.

Maria shut off the water and stepped from the shower. She donned the guest robe hanging on the back of the bathroom door, then rubbed moisturizer on her face and almond-scented lotion on her body. After confiscating a blow dryer from the vanity drawer, she styled her hair. When she entered the bedroom she found her cleaned clothes neatly folded on the bed. Maria dressed then ventured downstairs to the kitchen.

"Thank you for doing my laundry, Harriet." Maria smiled at the older woman who sat at the kitchen table sewing a button on a man's shirt.

"My pleasure." Harriet gestured to the coffeepot on the counter. "Help yourself."

"The Gateway is a beautiful ranch."

"Gil does a fine job taking care of it."

"Have you worked for Mr. Parker long?" Maria joined Harriet at the table.

"Most of my adult life. I was best friends with Gil's wife, Clare. When she died of breast cancer shortly after their son Eddy turned eight, I moved out here to help care for the house and my godson."

"You never married?"

"Never found a man who stole my heart." She knotted the thread.

Maria sipped her coffee and studied Harriet's features. She guessed the woman to be in her early sixties. Her skin was smooth with a few wrinkles around her eyes. Her salt-and-pepper bob flattered her heart-shaped face.

"What about you?" Harriet glanced at Maria's bare ring finger.

"I was engaged once."

"What happened?"

Divulging that her former fiancé had cheated on her was too painful so she settled for telling a half-truth. "Fernando changed his mind and decided he wanted children."

"You don't want to be a mother?"

"I work with delinquent teenagers and practically raise the kids myself. The last thing I want is to go home at the end of the day and have to take care of more kids."

"You'd feel differently toward your own flesh and blood."

Would she? Before Maria had become a teacher

she'd desired a family. Then her brother's death had shown Maria that parents' love for their child had the power to destroy them. "I wouldn't want to raise a child in the inner city where I live and work."

"You could move to the suburbs."

Harriet's suggestion made sense but the reason Maria was able to bond with her students was because she understood the challenges they faced—the 'hood was her home, too.

Needing to change the subject, Maria asked, "Can I help with the supper preparations?"

"I don't cook for the ranch hands. Pete does. He uses the kitchen attached to the bunkhouse."

"Are you joining everyone for supper?"

"No." Harriet packed away the sewing kit. "I prefer eating at the house, where I can control my portion size." She smiled.

"So I'm about to put on weight?" Maria took her mug to the sink.

"Pete makes the best cherry cobbler this side of the Mississippi. You'll be lucky if you get away with an extra pound or two."

"Thanks again for washing my clothes, Harriet. I enjoyed our chat."

"Stop in anytime."

When Maria left the house, she spotted Riley and the boys in the round pen with the bucking horse. She crept closer, then propped a boot on the lower rung and listened as Riley discussed the finer points of bustin' broncs.

"I don't get it," Alonso said. "How come you can't use both hands to hang on to the buck rein?"

"'Cause it would be too easy to stay on the bronc," Cruz said.

"Not only that," Riley said, "the cowboy can't touch the horse with his free hand. If he does, he's disqualified. And—" Riley patted the animal's shoulder "—you've got to mark the horse as he comes out of the chute."

"What does that mean?" Victor asked.

"When the chute opens, the cowboy has to keep his boot heels above the point of the horse's shoulder until the animal's front legs hit the ground."

"There's a lot to remember," Alonso said.

"You ride broncs long enough, it becomes second nature."

"What's a good score?" Cruz's interest in an activity other than tagging buildings and hanging out with gangs pleased Maria.

"Both the rider and the horse earn their own score—as much as twenty-five points each. The meaner the bronc and the nastier he bucks, the more points the horse and cowboy earn. A good score is in the high eighties."

Cruz strolled around the horse, stopping in front of the animal. "How old do you have to be to rodeo?"

"You're old enough right now to compete in junior rodeos. Once you're eighteen you can join the PRCA and buck against the best in the sport." When Cruz remained silent, Riley asked, "Want me to register you for a junior rodeo?"

"Maybe."

"Maybe you should see what your teacher thinks about you bustin' broncs."

"Hey, Ms. Alvarez." Alonso walked over to Maria. "Cruz might join the rodeo."

"I heard."

"Tell you what, Cruz," Riley said. "You and the

guys watch me compete next weekend in Las Vegas. Afterward, if you're interested in bustin' broncs—"

"Wait a minute," Maria waved a hand. "This isn't what Judge Hamel had in mind when she handed down Cruz's sentence."

"I wanna try rodeo, Ms. Alvarez." Cruz removed the straw cowboy hat given to him as part of his ranch uniform. "My father was good at it. Maybe I will be, too."

"What if Cruz makes a bargain with you?" Riley spoke to Maria.

"What kind of bargain?"

"If he continues with his studies and does his chores without complaining, I'll teach him how to bust broncs in his spare time. And…" Riley held Cruz's gaze. "I'll sponsor your first rodeo."

"What do you mean sponsor?" Cruz asked.

"I'll pay your entry fee and buy your rodeo gear."

"You'd do that for me?"

"On one condition," Riley said. "You earn your GED."

Out of the three boys, Cruz was furthest behind in his studies. He'd have to work long and hard to catch up to Alonso and Victor.

"Okay. I'll try," Cruz said.

"Trying isn't good enough. If you want to rodeo you'll pass your exams." Riley lowered his voice. "Do you want to bust broncs, kid?"

"Yeah, I want to rodeo." He spoke to Maria. "What if I can't learn the stuff?"

"I'll try to come out to the ranch more often to tutor you. In the meantime you keep up with the homework."

"Can we go with Riley to his next rodeo?" Victor asked.

Riley didn't allow Maria a chance to answer. "Your father called. The *Dark Stranger*'s ready to fly. We'd have to leave early in the morning next Friday and wouldn't return until Sunday night."

The boys begged for permission to accompany Riley to Vegas.

"What's the matter?" Riley asked Maria. "Are you afraid of flying?"

"Maybe."

"Flying's a breeze." Riley turned to the boys. "Have you guys flown before?"

All three shook their heads no.

"Then it will be an adventure for everyone. You'll love it, trust me."

Trust Riley? Easier said than done after watching him land his plane in the salvage yard. "I'll need to gain permission from the boys' parents and Judge Hamel." Maria prayed their answers would be no.

"How far is Las Vegas from Sioux Falls?" Cruz asked.

"It's about a thousand miles northeast of Vegas. Why? You want to go visit your father?" Riley said.

The teen shrugged. "Could you fly me there?"

"That's up to Ms. Alvarez." Riley glanced at Maria.

Maybe a visit with his father would convince Cruz to stay away from gangs and work harder to succeed in school. "I'll check into it," she said.

Right then a loud bell clanged. "Chow's ready. Go on. I'll meet you there," Riley said.

Why did Riley have to be one of the good guys, Maria wondered as she followed the boys to the mess hall.

"Riley's a cool dude," Cruz said.

"Yep, he's a—" *sexy, hot* "—cool dude," Maria concurred.

And very much off-limits.

Chapter Eight

Early Friday morning Maria and her father waited for Riley and the boys inside a hangar at the Blue Skies Regional Airport. Gaining her students' parents' permission, and in Cruz's case, Judge Hamel's, had been easy as pie. The parents were appreciative of their sons having an opportunity to travel outside New Mexico and Judge Hamel applauded Riley's involvement with the teens.

The judge had rambled on about how nice Riley was and how she wished there were more young men in the community willing to work with delinquent teens. Good grief, by the time Maria had left the judge's chambers Riley had sprouted wings and was well on his way to sainthood.

Maria wholeheartedly agreed with the judge's assessment of Riley, except for a tiny part of her that questioned his unselfish involvement in the boys' lives. Yes, Riley was a great guy—a well-mannered, mature, genuinely likable *young* man. But aside from "doing the right thing" what motivated Riley to help her students? Maria worried that *reason* was her.

Nonsense. She and Riley were attracted to one another but surely he understood they had no future together.

"Are you prepared for this, Maria?"

Her father's question referred to flying but Maria was thinking about what might happen between her and Riley in Vegas. "As long as you're certain the *Dark Stranger* won't drop out of the sky, I'll give flying a try."

"I tested the plane myself. You will have no trouble." Her father had kept his pilot's license current after he'd retired from the military, and often took planes on test flights to verify the repairs had been done correctly. "The *Dark Stranger* is a very expensive plane." Translation: Where does Riley get all his money?

"Riley's family raises Kentucky Derby horses."

When her father's eyes filled with suspicion, Maria wanted to shout, "I don't know why he's helping the boys" and "I don't know why he's interested in *me*—an older Hispanic woman from the 'hood," but she held her tongue.

"He's your brother's age."

"Juan is dead, Dad." Her father's mouth grimaced in pain and Maria regretted her words. Why couldn't her parents allow their son to rest in peace?

"You and this…cowboy…it's not proper."

Proper encompassed age, ethnicity, income and social standing.

"Dad, there's nothing going on between me and Riley. He's doing my students a favor, that's all."

"He's wasting his time on those boys. So are you. They're all the same—losers who don't respect human life."

"You're saying Juan was a loser, too, because he joined a gang?"

Her father's face turned ashen. There was plenty of blame to spread around for failing to notice signs that her brother had joined a gang. Maria had desperately wanted to make amends for failing Juan by helping young Hispanic teens. Each boy or girl she saved from a gang would not bring her brother back to life but they reaffirmed in Maria's mind and heart that Juan hadn't died in vain.

"Victor, Alonso and Cruz need a man to inspire them to succeed," she said.

"And a cowboy who throws his money around, flies an expensive jet, and buys anything he wants without working for it is the best person to show those boys how to make their way in life?"

Score a point for her father. Maria had contemplated the same thing after Riley had made arrangements for the teens to stay at the Gateway Ranch, but her doubts about his influence on her students had taken a backseat when she'd gotten sidetracked by her attraction to Riley.

The only way to break the cycle of poverty, drugs, gang violence and unemployment in the 'hood was through education. Would Riley throwing his money around encourage the boys to take a shortcut to fame and fortune? Unable to defend Riley against her father's criticism, she muttered, "He means well."

"You're too old to chase after—"

"I'm not chasing him." Maria curled her fingers into a fist. She'd been devastated when Fernando had ended their relationship. Riley's interest in her—although temporary—was a desperately needed boost to her feminine ego. "We're friends. That's it."

Maria kept her eyes on the airport entrance across the runway, longing for Riley to arrive and put an end to the sparring between her and her father. A moment later, she got her wish. "They're here."

Riley parked in the visitor lot then he and the boys entered the hangar. He removed his sunglasses and grinned. Lord, Maria would miss his smile when he moved on and out of her life.

Each of the boys carried a black leather duffel bag with the Gateway Ranch logo stamped on the side. Riley held out his hand to Maria's father. "How are you, Mr. Alvarez?" He didn't wait for a response before motioning to the plane. "The *Dark Stranger* looks as good as new." Riley walked over to the plane, the boys trailing behind, listening to her father's explanation of the repairs that had been made to the plane.

"Has anyone taken it on a test flight?" Riley asked.

"I flew the plane myself," Maria's father said.

"Great. I'll settle the bill for repairs, file a flight plan, then we'll be on our way." Riley turned to the boys. "You guys board the plane, but stay out of the cockpit." He opened the door and pulled down the stairs. "Ms. Alvarez—" he smiled at Maria "—gets to be my copilot."

"I think I should sit in the back with the boys." *And cross my fingers until we land.*

"First-time fliers fair better in the cockpit." Riley directed his next words to her father. "Isn't that right, Mr. Alvarez?"

Murmuring that he needed to get the paperwork ready, Maria's father walked off and Riley followed. He hadn't imagined the tension between father and daughter when he'd entered the hangar. What had the two talked about before he'd arrived? As much as he respected Ricardo Alvarez and his mechanical talents,

Riley sensed the man didn't trust him around Maria. He stepped into the office and shut the door.

"Mr. Alvarez, I want to thank you again for working on my plane." Ricardo handed Riley the work order. He scanned the list of parts ordered, the cost of towing the plane to the airport and Ricardo's fee for labor. "This can't be correct."

"I charged you the going rate."

"You worked on my plane after-hours and on the weekend. That's overtime. This bill should be double the amount."

Ricardo scowled.

Stalemate. Riley waited, hoping the older man would back down. When he remained silent, Riley said, "I won't sign off on this until you change the amount."

Ricardo snatched the paperwork out of Riley's hand, crossed out the total and added two hundred dollars, not nearly enough but Riley suspected this was as far as Ricardo would budge. Riley removed his checkbook from his shirt pocket and made out a draft for the repairs. "Thank you again for taking good care of my plane."

"Don't hurt my daughter."

The statement shocked Riley. "Excuse me?"

"I see the way you stare at her. You're not her kind and—"

"Kind? You mean because I'm a rodeo cowboy or because I'm white?"

"Both."

Experiencing prejudice was a first for Riley.

"And you are too young for Maria." Ricardo's lip curled. "The wealthy believe they can buy anything and everyone they want. My daughter isn't for sale."

Not wanting to argue, Riley spoke in an even tone. "I'm helping Maria with her students. There's no reason we can't be friends and enjoy each other's company."

"So you want an affair with her and then you disappear?"

Temper flaring, Riley picked his words carefully. "My relationship with your daughter is none of your business. Maria's old enough to know who she wants or doesn't want. She's a beautiful, giving, generous, kind woman. Any man, no matter what his age or race, would consider himself lucky to have her in his life."

"You're too young to know your own mind."

Tired of having his age held against him, Riley said, "Mr. Alvarez, I care a lot for your daughter but frankly it doesn't matter if you approve of me or not." He left the office, closing the door quietly behind him. Shoot. This wasn't how he'd planned to begin the trip to Nevada. Riley hoped Maria's father hadn't convinced her to keep her distance from him in Vegas, because he wanted the trip to be the beginning of a long-term relationship between them. As soon as the *Dark Stranger* was airborne, Riley would focus all his efforts on showing Maria and the boys a good time.

Don't forget about the rodeo.

Riley had become so involved with Maria and her students that he was losing track of his rodeo goals. He needed a win this weekend. Once he boarded the plane, he secured the cabin door. "What do you think?" he asked the teens.

"Sweet!" Alonso said, examining the compartments around his seat.

"Fasten your belts and stay seated until I say it's

okay to move around." He sent the boys a stern look. "I'm serious."

"Yeah, okay," Cruz said.

"Ready?" Riley asked when he entered the cockpit.

"As ready as I'll ever be." Maria smiled but her eyes remained sober.

Riley slipped into the pilot's chair. "You're going to love flying."

"If I don't?"

"I'll put you on a bus back to Albuquerque as soon as the rodeo's over and the boys and I will be waiting for you when you arrive at the terminal downtown."

"Gee, thanks."

With quick, efficient movements Riley ran through his preflight checklist. Five minutes later he flipped on the intercom. "Okay, guys, we're set to leave as soon as the tower gives us permission." A chorus of "okays" echoed from the back of the plane.

Once Riley received the go-ahead to taxi onto the runway he watched the propeller blades rotate smoothly and evenly. "Your father does good work."

"He's the best around."

The tower cleared him for takeoff and the plane's ascent into the sky was smooth and quick. Hoping to avoid another bird strike, Riley climbed to ten thousand feet, then leveled off and informed the boys they were free to unfasten their seat belts.

"You can let go now," he said.

Maria relaxed her tightly entwined fingers. "It's peaceful at this altitude. I bet this is what Heaven feels like."

Was she thinking about her brother? Riley didn't care for the fact that he and Juan—had the teenager lived—would have been the same age. Riley hoped once they arrived in Vegas, Maria would become too distracted to ponder anything but having a good time with him and the boys.

Riley had two goals in Vegas—to win first place in the bronc-bustin' competition and to show Maria that his feelings for her were serious. If he'd learned anything the past two weeks at the Gateway Ranch it was that he wanted to be more than friends with the inner-city schoolteacher.

"WHOA, WE'RE STAYING HERE?" Alonso said, his face pressed against the window in the backseat of the cab.

The driver stopped outside the entrance of the New York-New York Hotel and Casino on the Las Vegas strip. The exterior of the hotel reflected the New York City skyline...on a much smaller scale. The hotel towers had been configured to resemble the Empire State Building and the Chrysler Building, and the lake in front of the property represented New York Harbor. The hotel also included mock replicas of the Statue of Liberty, Ellis Island and Grand Central Station.

The cab ride from the municipal airport had started out boisterous but the closer they'd driven to the strip the quieter the teens had become. None of them, including Maria, had ever been to Vegas and their wide-eyed gapes seemed to amuse Riley.

"Do they keep the lights on all the time?" Victor asked as Riley paid the cab fare.

"Unless there's a power outage, the lights never dim in Vegas."

The boys piled out of the cab and retrieved their duffel bags from the trunk. A bellman appeared with a luggage cart. "Welcome back to the New York-New

York, Mr. Fitzgerald." The young man tipped his cap. "Good luck today at the rodeo."

"Thanks, Mike. You coming to watch the events?"

"Yes, sir. Only a fool would miss a chance to mingle with all those pretty buckle bunnies."

Buckle bunnies set off a warning buzzer inside Maria's head. Until now she'd managed to avoid contemplating that part of rodeo.

"Same suite, Mr. Fitzgerald?"

"Yep." Riley placed a folded bill in the young man's palm.

"Thank you, sir. Enjoy your stay." The bellman bowed, then steered the cart inside the hotel.

"How much does that guy make in tips?" Victor asked.

"I'd guess on a good day two to three hundred dollars."

Victor whistled between his teeth.

"Before you get any ideas about running off to Vegas and becoming a bellman, you should know that Mike graduated from high school and is studying hotel management at the university."

"How come you know so much about the guy?" Cruz asked.

"I stay at the New York-New York when I'm in Vegas. Mike and I talk about sports at my alma mater."

Maria considered it odd that Riley gave the time of day to a recently graduated high school student, until she realized that Riley was fairly close in age to Mike.

"Ready to ride a roller coaster?" Riley asked.

"Where?" Alonso asked.

"Right here in the hotel." Riley pointed to the sky. A red coaster snaked through the mock Manhattan skyline.

"I'm in," Victor said.

"Me, too," Cruz and Alonso echoed.

"What about you, Maria?" Riley asked.

"I don't like roller coasters." The bends and turns made her stomach queasy.

"You'll like this one." Riley grabbed her hand. "The loading station is inside the building at the rear of the casino."

As they made their way through the maze of gaming tables and slot machines, the boys asked Riley how many times he'd ridden the coaster and what he thought of the experience. Maria was grateful Riley hadn't released her hand as he described the terrifying ride.

I can do this. Maria refused to put a damper on the boys' excitement because she was afraid of heights. The boarding area for the ride resembled a mini New York subway station. She released Riley's hand to retrieve her wallet.

"I'm paying." Riley got in line at the ticket booth.

"This is crazy, Ms. Alvarez." Alonso could barely contain his excitement. The ride attendant secured passengers in taxicab cars. Any ride that needed over-the-shoulder harnesses and side-to-side head restraints promised a bruising experience.

"Here." Victor shoved a brochure into Maria's hand.

"Thanks," she mumbled, daring herself to read the literature.

Let the good times roll. The Roller Coaster will lift you up 203 feet, drop you down 144 feet at speeds up to 67 mph. Simulating a jet fighter's barrel roll, you'll turn 180 degrees, hang 86 feet in the air, take the famous "heartline" twist and dive and get your negative G's on! Enjoy the rush!

Rush? How about heart attack?

"We've got an odd number of riders," Riley said when he returned. Before Maria volunteered to sit out, he asked, "Who wants to ride alone?"

"Me." Cruz raised his hand in the air.

As the line snaked through the turnstiles, Maria said, "Are you sure this is a good idea right before you compete?"

Riley smiled. "You're scared."

Of course she was frightened! Any sane person would be leery of riding a roller coaster that zigzagged through a miniature New York City.

"You won't fall out." Riley slipped his arm around her and Maria resisted hugging him back. "I'll keep you safe."

When their turn came to board the coaster, Maria chose the inside seat and checked twice to make sure the harness and lap belt were secured then she closed her eyes and focused on the seductive scent of Riley's cologne.

"You're not going to keep your eyes shut the entire ride, are you?" he asked.

"Yes, I am."

"If you're this scared, why did you agree to ride the coaster?"

"I didn't want to disappoint the boys." *And I didn't want you to think I was a boring person.*

The taxicab lurched forward and another group boarded. A few seconds later the attendant's voice bellowed over the intercom. "Ladies and gentlemen, prepare for the ride of your life. Please remain seated until your taxicab returns to the station." A whistle blew. "See you back here in two minutes and forty-five seconds!"

The cars climbed the track, and Maria clutched the shoulder harness until her fingers hurt. The boys raised their hands in the air, shouting dares at each other. As the taxicab neared the summit Maria took in the aerial view of the south end of the strip, where Las Vegas Boulevard met Tropicana Avenue.

The sight lasted only a few seconds before the car plummeted one hundred and forty-four feet, sending her stomach slamming into her throat. Maria became a human pinball as the coaster hung her upside down then flung her through loops and corkscrew turns. She prayed the operator would cut the ride short but the blasted whirlwind experience lasted a lifetime before the train's brakes jerked the ride to a stop inside Grand Central Station.

"Man, that was awesome!" Victor said.

"You hung on when we were upside down," Cruz accused Alonso.

"No way, dude, I let go…for a second." The boys laughed.

Despite the little aches and twinges—souvenirs from the ride—Maria basked in the moment, enjoying the boys' excitement. For the first time since she'd met the teens they acted like typical seventeen-year-olds—friends bantering good-naturedly. A nice change from their usual threatening scowls and I-dare-you glares.

"Did you like the ride, Ms. Alvarez?" Victor asked.

"Awesome." Maria ignored Riley's chuckle in her ear.

"Can we go again?" Cruz asked.

"I've got to head over to the arena, but we'll ride the coaster tonight after the rodeo." Riley led the way to the hotel lobby and secured key cards for their rooms. The elevator stopped on the tenth floor. "You guys are sharing the Skyline Room. The bellhop will deliver a roll-away bed while we're at the rodeo." Riley slid the key card into the lock and opened the door. The boys rushed in to check out the room.

Victor went straight for one of the queen-size beds and flung himself onto the mattress. "I call this bed!"

Alonso took a step toward the other bed but Cruz cut him off at the pass. "No, way, dude. This bed's mine."

"Doesn't matter," Alonso said. "The roll-away will be better than the hard bunks we sleep in at the ranch."

Maria tugged Riley's shirtsleeve. "Where are you sleeping?"

"I've got a single room." Riley pointed to the connecting door on his left.

"Where am I sleeping?"

He motioned to another connecting door on Maria's right. "You're on the other side of the boys' room in the Spa Suite."

Spa suite sounded heavenly. She didn't care to guess how much the rooms had cost Riley.

"We're leaving in twenty minutes," Riley told the teens, then walked Maria to her door and handed her the key card. "The guys and I will meet you in the lobby."

Maria snagged his arm as he turned away. "I can't thank you enough for what you're doing for the boys." *And me.*

"I'm glad you're here, Maria. It's nice not having to travel alone for a change."

She slipped into her room, freshened up then took the elevator to the lobby, where they all piled into a cab and drove along Vegas Boulevard to Mesquite Avenue.

"Hey!" Victor exclaimed. "A carnival. Can we go on the rides?"

"Maybe later," Riley said. "Let's grab supper before the parade kicks off. My event isn't until nine o'clock tonight."

"Everyone hungry?" Maria asked.

"We're always hungry, Ms. Alvarez," Alonso said.

The cab dropped them off at the rodeo grounds, where Riley paid their admission and they got their hands stamped.

"The ink disappeared," Victor complained to the gate attendant who'd stamped the back of his hand.

"It glows in the dark, kid." The man pointed a special light, which revealed the green ink splotch.

They zigzagged through the growing throng of people and made their way to the food vendors. Riley told the boys to eat as much as they wanted. Maria was grateful the teens kept their orders reasonable— chili-cheese dogs, fries and drinks. *When in Rome...* She ordered the same, hoping she'd walk off the extra calories by the end of the day.

"What happens next?" Alonso asked Riley after they found a picnic table in the eating area. Maria noticed Cruz studying the rodeo cowboys milling about.

"I'll give you guys a tour of the livestock pens then we'll head over to Fourth Street for the parade."

"Won't you be tired after all that walking?" Maria asked.

"I'll be fine." Spoken like a true twenty-five-year-old. "Once the parade ends, I return to the cowboy-ready area and—"

"What's a cowboy-ready area?" Cruz asked.

"Where cowboys put on their gear," Riley said. "While I'm doing that, you can find seats in the stands."

"You gonna win tonight?" Victor asked.

"I'd better since you came all this way to watch me." Riley spoke to the boys—the double meaning behind his words not lost on Maria.

Not only did Riley intend to win his rodeo event tonight… But he also intended to win *her*.

Chapter Nine

As far as parades went the Helldorado Days event sponsored by the Elks Club was a big hit with the Las Vegas locals, but drew few tourists, who preferred to remain in the casinos and give their money to the great state of Nevada.

Riley, Maria and the boys stood on Fourth Street at the corner of Ogden Avenue near the rodeo grounds. The parade consisted of relic cars displaying ads for local businesses and walking teams wearing themed clothing—Civil War uniforms, Southern-belle dresses, old-West gunslingers and lawmen outfits. The rodeo clowns had dressed early for the event and entertained the kids lined along the sidewalks.

Cruz, Alonso and Victor acted as if the festivities bored them but Riley caught the teens pointing at people in the parade, cracking jokes and laughing. Maria's mood was difficult to judge. She'd been polite but distant toward him since they'd left the hotel. Riley couldn't figure out what he'd done to cause the sudden shift in her demeanor. Her behavior made him feel less than her equal—not in age but maturity—and he didn't appreciate it.

This wasn't the first time Maria acted older than

her thirty-five years. Riley blamed her matronly attitude on having lived in the trenches of Albuquerque. Kids in the 'hood matured fast, and the death of Maria's brother to gang violence had left her with deep scars. Riley's upbringing was worlds apart from Maria's, which made their perspectives different. But the very experiences Maria had lived through had molded her into the woman she was today—the woman Riley desired.

He understood her need to help delinquent teens and he admired and envied her noble calling; but a part of Riley wished he could erase her past so that nothing but ten years stood between them. He'd proven they could have fun together. Laugh together. Enjoy each other's company. Add sexual attraction to the mix and Riley believed they were the perfect pair.

"What are you staring at?"

"You have chili-dog sauce on your cheek." He leaned in close. "Want me to lick it off?"

"Stop that," she whispered, the sparkle in her eyes taking the sting out of her threat.

A sudden blast of music ended the intimate moment. One after the other, local high-school bands marched down the street followed by their school float. Centennial High's float consisted of their football team in full uniform with the school mascot—a bulldog—sitting on a cardboard throne, wearing a crown. The sign pinned to the side of the flatbed trailer listed numerous state championships.

The Coronado High float sported a large cougar head, which rotated in a slow circle while red, white and blue streamers decorated the sides of the trailer. Students wore fifties clothing and danced to Elvis's "Jailhouse Rock."

Eldorado High decorated their float in maroon and gold. One student wearing a Sun Devil costume held a pitchfork above his head. The other students dressed in T-shirts with a picture of their mascot on the front.

The cowboy was Chaparral High School's talisman. The students wore ten-gallon hats, Wranglers and orange-and-black bandanas around their necks.

A red Dodge Ram pulled the final float in the parade—a flatbed covered in sawdust, crowded with buckle bunnies vying for a turn on the mechanical bull that slowly gyrated in the center of the trailer. Cat calls and wolf whistles greeted the float.

As the pickup passed, the blonde swaying atop the bull made eye contact with Riley. He mumbled a curse. Victoria was a casino waitress by day and a rodeo groupie by night. He stepped behind Cruz, hoping the kid would hide him from view. He hadn't been quick enough.

Victoria's whiney voice rang through the air. "Wanna party, Riley?"

Damn. Right when he'd coaxed a smile out of Maria, the buckle bunny had to come along and ruin his progress.

"Hey, Riley," Cruz said. "If you don't wanna party with that chick, I will." The boys chuckled.

Face heating, Riley ignored Victoria. Maria's hot stare was more difficult to discount. "Well?" She nudged him with her elbow.

Play dumb. "Well what?"

"Are you going to party with that bimbo later?"

This was the first time Maria had revealed a jealous streak. "Victoria and I..." Riley clamped his mouth closed when he caught the boys eavesdropping.

"Hey," Cruz said. "I'm serious about the girl. If you don't want her—"

Maria tapped the back of Cruz's head with her open palm. "No hooking up with girls while we're in Vegas. Got that?"

A chorus of "Yes, ma'am" answered.

"That's it for the parade." Hoping to avoid a run-in with Victoria, Riley rushed everyone over to the rodeo grounds. When they arrived at the bucking chutes, he asked, "You guys want to see the horses and the bulls?"

"Yeah, sure," Victor said.

"You're welcome to come, but there's a lot of cussing and spitting behind the chutes," Riley teased Maria.

"Thanks, I'll wait in the stands." Maria pointed to the bleachers on the right side of the arena. "I'll sit near the top."

"Here." Riley removed his watch and handed it to her. "Will you keep this for me?"

"Sure." Maria studied the timepiece, noting the expensive platinum coating and crystal glass under which a cowboy on a bucking horse pointed to the hour and minutes. The watch appeared custom-made. Her jeans were too tight to stow the jewelry in her pocket so she wore it.

As soon as the guys walked off, Maria made her way into the stands. By the time she reached the top bleachers she was gasping for air. She watched a TV broadcaster interview a cowboy near the VIP seating section, then switched her attention to the flag girls practicing their routine while a rodeo crew assembled a platform in the center of the arena.

The stands filled quickly. A beautiful redhead, wearing a tight T-shirt, leather-fringed vest, painted-on jeans with a flashy rhinestone belt and shiny black boots, sat a few feet down from Maria.

She'd never been self-conscious of her physical appearance but one trip to a rodeo and suddenly she was surrounded by hordes of beautiful, flamboyant, young women. She felt drab by comparison.

They may have beauty but you have brains.

The thought did little to lift her spirits.

The redhead's smile froze when she glanced at Maria's wrist. "May I ask where you got that?"

For a moment Maria had forgotten about Riley's watch. "Oh, it's not mine. I'm keeping it for—"

"Riley Fitzgerald?"

The blood drained from Maria's face and she struggled to keep her smile in place. "Yes. As a matter of fact it belongs to Riley."

"I used to keep it for him when he rode."

Oh, Lord. She should have expected she'd run into one of Riley's ex's. "How long ago was that?"

"College. We split before graduation." The soft sigh following the statement hinted that Riley had broken the redhead's heart.

"Please don't take offense," the young woman said, flashing a sweet smile, "but you're not Riley's usual type."

Her comment burned Maria like a nasty wasp sting. "We're friends."

The redhead's expression lightened. "Is he dating anyone special?"

Me, Maria wanted to shout. She knew Riley flew his own plane and came from Kentucky. He'd been born into a wealthy family and attended college at UNLV. He'd won a world title in saddle-bronc riding. But as far as his personal life...Maria knew next to nothing.

Maybe Riley had left a string of broken hearts across the country. The moment the thought entered her mind, she regretted it.

She considered herself a good judge of character and Riley was a kind, decent, caring man. No matter that Maria fabricated excuses for their attraction to one another, she believed Riley's intentions toward her—whatever they were—were honest and sincere. If only the odds of a lasting relationship between them were better than slim-to-none.

"Riley's not involved with anyone that I know of at the moment." Maria didn't count herself because she and Riley weren't having sex.

"I'm Amy, by the way."

"Maria."

"Do you live here in Vegas?"

"Albuquerque. I'm a teacher. I help juvenile offenders earn their GEDs."

"Your career sounds challenging," Amy said. "I'm a pediatric nurse. My father wanted me to go to law school then work for him in his firm, but I was interested in the medical field."

"Law doesn't appeal to you?"

"Dad's a pretty famous divorce attorney in Vegas and I've watched him take his clients' spouses to the cleaners. I'm afraid I'm not that cutthroat. I'd rather help people heal, not inflict more wounds."

"I understand the wanting to make a difference in someone's life." Maria regretted that she'd misjudged Amy and had lumped her in with all the other airheads at the rodeo. She yearned to know why Amy and Riley had ended their relationship, but lost her chance to ask when the boys appeared.

"Hey, Ms. Alvarez! We got you nachos!" Alonso

led the charge up the bleachers. The boys stopped at the end of the aisle and gaped at Amy.

"Guys—" Maria grabbed the nacho container before it slipped from Alonso's hand "—this is a friend of Riley's. Amy…?"

"Amy Reynolds."

Cruz introduced himself first. Alonso and Victor followed then sat in the row in front of Amy. The boys talked excitedly about the bucking stock they'd seen and the cowboys Riley had introduced them to.

"Ms. Alvarez, we got to meet Mr. Parker's son, Ed," Alonso said.

"Ed told us when he was a kid he used to feed his dad's horse broccoli because it made the horse fart when his dad rode him." Victor jabbed Cruz in the side. "Hey. We should feed Shorty's horse—"

"There will be no feeding broccoli to any horses at the ranch," Maria said.

The teens bobbed their heads.

"How many students do you have?" Amy asked.

"I'm helping sixteen at the moment. Much of the work is self-paced." She waggled a finger at the boys. "Riley arranged for them to work at the Gateway Ranch north of Albuquerque while they earn their GEDs." Maria lowered her voice. "The boys were associating with a local gang and at risk of dropping out of the program."

"Typical Riley," Amy said.

"He has a big heart." And Maria envied the lucky woman who would one day lay claim to it.

"You don't have to convince me. When I was doing my nursing clinicals, Riley helped me throw a birthday party for one of my terminally ill patients—a little boy who wanted to be a rodeo cowboy when he grew up.

Riley brought in a clown to entertain the kids and he
gave bull-riding lessons on a mechanical bull." Amy's
smile vanished. "Santiago died two weeks later. Riley
and I went to his funeral."

Maria's eyes stung. The more she learned about
Riley the more her heart craved to pull him close. Amy
Reynolds appeared to be the perfect match for Riley.
They were both attractive, educated and came from
well-to-do-families. Why wasn't Riley with Amy?

Maybe he's commitment-shy.

Right then the rodeo kicked off. The mayor gave
a welcome speech and two girls—one carrying the
American flag, the other the Nevada state flag—
raced into the arena on horseback. They stopped their
mounts in front of the stands. The spectators stood and
a young man with a baritone voice belted out the national anthem.

Once the applause died down, the announcer introduced the rodeo sponsors. The people waved from
their leather chairs in the VIP section near the bucking
chutes. The bullfighters and pickup men were named
next, then the clowns and finally the rodeo queen and
her court.

"Ladies and gents, welcome to the Helldorado Day's
Rodeo! Tonight you're gonna see the finest bucking
stock in Nevada and the best-known cowboys on the
circuit competing for thousands of dollars in prize
money."

The rodeo clowns strutted in front of the crowd,
staggering under the weight of a giant-size cardboard
check. The announcer droned on about the evening's
events but Maria's thoughts were elsewhere until she
heard Riley's name.

"We got last year's world champion in saddle-bronc

riding here tonight! Riley Fitzgerald from Lexington, Kentucky."

Amy popped off the bench, stuck her fingers between her lips and let out a shrill whistle. Thunderous applause boomed through the stands and the boys glanced around in shock. Maria had no idea Riley was so popular with fans.

"You may have heard Fitzgerald won the title by default when Drew Rawlins scratched the final ride of his career here in Las Vegas last December. I spoke with Fitzgerald earlier and that young man's on a mission to claim a second title. Keep your eye on him tonight."

Amy sat down. "When Riley competed with the rodeo team in college he drew big crowds and lots of pretty girls."

"Did that ever bother you?" Maria asked.

"Sure it did. That's why we split."

Don't ask. Another voice in her head said…*ask.* Curiosity got the best of her. "Did he cheat on you?"

"Yes."

The bottom fell out of Maria's stomach.

"Groupies drooled all over his boots everywhere he went. I couldn't compete with so many girls."

Any fantasy Maria had entertained about her and Riley becoming more than friends died a quick death. Her ex, Fernando, had been seeing a woman on the side for six months before he'd ended his relationship with Maria—and only because he'd gotten the woman pregnant. Infidelity hurt no matter what the person's age.

This newest tidbit of gossip about Riley confirmed Maria's earlier suspicion that when it came to helping others, Riley was a swell guy. But as far as a personal relationship with him, Maria was convinced it would end in heartache—hers.

"Riley's event is next." Amy clasped her hands together. "I hope he wins."

How was it that Riley had broken Amy's heart, yet she cared enough about him to want him to do well? *Good grief.* What kind of magic spell did the cowboy cast over females? Maria wished she'd never run in to Amy today. Ignorance was bliss. Now that she understood it was all about the chase for Riley, Maria refused to get caught.

Feeling confident in her decision to keep her relationship with Riley on the lighter side Maria joined forces with Amy, praying Riley would win his event.

"My OLD MAN NEVER SAID A word about letting delinquent teens work at the Gateway Ranch." Ed Parker stood next to Riley in the cowboy-ready area.

"How long since you last spoke to your dad?" Riley asked.

"A month maybe."

"The boys have been at the ranch a few weeks now." Riley rummaged through his gear bag. "Your dad's got a big heart. Cruz, Alonso and Victor might turn their life around because he's giving them a place to learn what hard work is all about."

Parker stubbed his boot tip against the ground, but didn't speak.

"Your dad misses you," Riley said.

The comment startled Parker. "He said that?"

"Didn't have to. I saw it in his eyes."

"He misses his granddaughter." Parker's shoulders slumped. "My ex took Shelly out to California with her to live with her parents."

"I'm sorry." Riley had heard the same story from more than one cowboy on the circuit. They got a buckle bunny pregnant, married her and then divorced within a year. No way was Riley heading down that path. If and when he decided to marry, his rodeo career would be over.

"Heard you drew Houdini. He won big in Oklahoma last month," Parker said.

He needed a win the first go-round. Riley counted on Houdini's brand of magic bringing him success tonight.

"You listening to the gossip behind the chutes?" Ed asked.

Riley's competitors were jealous. If the boot was on the other foot he'd feel the same. Riley fastened his chaps. "What's everybody saying this time?"

"Nick Bass thinks because you're rich you're a pansy." The twenty-nine-year-old bronc rider stood by himself next to his chute.

Bass was a loner who'd joined the circuit late in the season. He had talent, but if he didn't learn to control his anger, he'd never succeed at the sport. Riley knew for a fact that Bass had grown up dirt-poor and held a grudge against wealthy people. The man was as raw on the inside as he was on the outside.

"Never mind Bass," Riley said. "He can't focus worth a damn."

Speaking of concentrating, Riley waged his own battle as his thoughts drifted to Maria. He ached to sneak off alone with her tonight. He wanted Maria as badly as he wanted to make it to eight on Houdini. Riley glanced toward the stands, searching for her and the boys. As he scanned the rows his eyes landed on a redheaded vixen. *Amy?* He groaned.

"What's the matter?" Parker asked.

"Nothing." Riley hadn't thought of Amy in forever. Even so he was ashamed of how his relationship with his college flame had ended. That she sat next to Maria didn't bode well for him. The last thing he needed was a confrontation with Amy when he was trying to set a spark to his and Maria's relationship. He feared his plan to light Maria's fire tonight was dying a slow death in the stands.

"Good luck." Parker straightened his hat then walked off to prepare for his own ride.

Riley closed his eyes, willing his mind to empty of women. Once his skull rang hollow, he harnessed his energy, turning it inward. Then he gave himself a pep talk.

Don't loosen your grip on the buck rein when Houdini busts out of the chute.

Don't try to outthink Houdini. Follow his lead.

Keep your spurs above the shoulder points and roll 'em slow and steady.

Remember Houdini turns to his right. Be ready but stay loose.

Maria's watching.

Win.

"Good luck, hoss."

A second after the words were spoken, Riley felt a hard slap against his shoulder and, unprepared for the blow, he stumbled forward. He glared at his nemesis, Stover. "I'm feelin' lucky tonight. How about you?"

"This is Vegas. We're all feelin' lucky." Stover sauntered off.

Riley engaged Houdini in a stare down. "You're not throwin' me, you sorry excuse for a bronc."

Houdini neighed.

"Folks, turn your eyes to chute number eight. Riley Fitzgerald from Lexington, Kentucky, is gonna open tonight's bronc-bustin' competition by performing a magic trick on Houdini!" The announcer snickered at his joke.

Riley climbed the chute rails and swung a leg over the gelding, then settled low in the saddle. He tugged at his riding glove before grabbing the buck rein. He worked the leather between his fingers, familiarizing himself with the rope.

Houdini didn't twitch a muscle.

Retreating deep inside himself Riley followed the same routine he'd developed in college—even, quiet breaths. Squeezing the rope then loosening his grip— five times in a row. He attempted to picture his mother, father and sister, but instead saw Maria's pretty brown eyes.

A surge of adrenaline pumped through his veins. This was his chance to show Maria he wasn't playing at being a rodeo cowboy. He was a man on a mission. A man with a goal. A man with skill, maturity and a talent for rodeo.

One. Two. Three. Riley nodded to the gateman. The chute door opened and Houdini vaulted from the gates. Riley set his spurs high against the horse's shoulders until the bronc landed on all four hooves after his first buck. He clenched the rein tighter.

Houdini was unpredictable and threw trick after trick at his riders. The bronc spun to the right in tight circles, blurring the stands before Riley's eyes. He nudged Houdini's right flank with his spur and the bronc made Riley pay. Houdini back-jumped, slamming his hooves into the dirt. Excruciating pain radiated up Riley's spine and into his brain. He'd have a hell of a backache tomorrow.

The pain intensified when Houdini's head swung right while his body curled left, forcing Riley's hips to twist awkwardly. The muscles in his thighs burned. Sweat stung his eyes.

Riley had never gotten into the habit of counting to eight during his ride—mainly because it interfered with his concentration. Right now he wished to hell he knew how many seconds had passed since the gate had opened, because it felt as if he and the horse had been dancing in the dirt for hours.

Houdini saved his best for last—a vertical jump that would have unseated most veteran cowboys. No way was Riley being thrown tonight—not with Maria and the boys as witnesses.

The buzzer blew and he wasted no time unraveling the buck rein from around his hand. Riley was known for his acrobatic dismounts—he and his college buddies had worked hard to perfect the stunts. He continued to ride Houdini, waiting for the right buck. Riley released the rope and swung his left leg over Houdini's head before leaping to the ground. He landed on both feet, then sprang forward into a front flip. His hat popped off his head, but Riley landed upright and extended his arm, snatching the Stetson before it landed in the dirt.

The crowd went wild.

Riley waved his hat to where Maria and the boys sat then bowed, which caused the fans to erupt in a second round of boot-stomping and cheers.

"There you have it, folks. Riley Fitzgerald's eighty-seven is the score to beat tonight. That young man sure knows how to entertain!"

"You're nothing but a showoff, kid," Stover said when Riley returned to the cowboy-ready area.

"You beat my score and I'll lick your boots."

Stover didn't have a chance of winning tonight. The man had drawn Black Velvet—a dink. Even if Stover performed well, his horse wouldn't, which put the cowboy out of the running for the championship round on Sunday.

"Careful what you say, Fitzgerald. You might be ridin' Black Velvet one of these days." Disgusted, Stover stomped away.

Riley had had enough of rodeo for one day. His back screamed for a soak in a hot tub—specifically the one in Maria's room. He stuffed his riding gear into the bag and headed for the stands. As far as he was concerned, his best ride was yet to come.

Chapter Ten

Riley waited for the roller coaster to return Victor, Cruz and Alonso to the mock train station in the New York-New York Hotel. After the rodeo he'd met up with the boys and Maria—thank God Amy hadn't stuck around to speak to him. But the damage had been done. Maria hadn't shown any enthusiasm when she'd congratulated Riley on his win. He guessed she'd discovered he and Amy had dated in the past, but he held out hope that his former girlfriend had spared Maria the details of his infidelity.

Instead of tagging along with him and the boys to the roller coaster, Maria had returned to her room, citing exhaustion. Needing time to devise a game plan to finagle an invitation into her suite, he'd offered to take the boys to the roller coaster before the ride shut down for the night. After three consecutive runs, the teens relinquished their seats in the taxicab cars.

"You sure you don't wanna ride?" Victor asked Riley when they stepped onto the platform.

"Nah, I'm wiped from the rodeo." Houdini had done a number on Riley's back. What he wouldn't give right now to feel Maria's deft fingers massaging his tight, achy muscles. "C'mon. I'll buy you guys a snack at the pizzeria."

"Can we watch a pay-per-view movie?" Victor asked.

"As long as you keep it R-rated. No porn." Riley hated to see Maria get into trouble if word reached Judge Hamel that the boys had watched X-rated movies in the hotel room.

"We've seen titty shows before," Cruz said.

The patrons at a gaming table stared as the boys passed. "Keep your voices down," Riley said.

"We're not virgins," Cruz grumbled.

Riley figured the teens had already experimented with sex, but *this* road trip would be nothing but clean fun—for the boys, that is. "No porn."

They stopped at the New York Pizzeria restaurant and Riley ordered an extra-large sausage-and-cheese pie, pretzel knots and quart-sized sodas, hoping the food would fill the teens until the following morning. Once they returned to the room and dug into the pizza, Riley checked on Maria.

What do I say? Riley hovered in front of Maria's door, struggling with opening lines.

I made a mistake.

I didn't mean to cheat.

I'd planned to break up with Amy anyway. His insides recoiled at the pathetic excuse even though it had been the honest-to-God truth.

Feeling as if he'd lost the round before the opening bell, Riley rapped his knuckles against the door.

"Who's there?"

"It's me, Riley."

The door widened a crack and Maria peeked at him. "Are you and the boys in for the night?"

"Yeah. They're eating pizza and watching a movie."

"What time should I be ready tomorrow?"

Ignoring the question, he asked, "Mind if I come in for a few minutes?"

The door closed and she released the security chain before waving him inside. The air in the suite was humid and heavy with the scent of perfumed soap. He stopped in the middle of the room and faced Maria.

She wore the white hotel robe found in all the bathrooms. He glanced at the hot tub, which sat outside the bathroom, facing the windows that overlooked the strip. The curtains remained open and he guessed she'd dimmed the lights and enjoyed the glittery Vegas skyline while sitting in the tub. "How was your bath?"

"Relaxing." Her mouth curved in a soft smile. "Wish I had one of these at home."

"I rent this room when I compete in Vegas. The hot tub comes in handy after each ride." He rubbed his palm against his lower back.

"Did you get hurt today?" Her eyes wandered over his body, and Riley felt a pang of arousal tug low in his gut.

"Spine's a little stiff. Mind if I take a soak?" As long as they were dancing around the subject, Riley might as well ease his sore muscles.

"Sure. I'll wait in the casino until you're finished." She grabbed her clothes from the back of a chair and rushed toward the bathroom.

Riley stopped her with a hand on her waist. "Don't leave."

Tiny pulses of electricity spread through Maria's abdomen when Riley tightened his fingers against her hipbone. She wanted to stay. She wanted to leave.

She didn't know what she wanted.

He leaned in, his lips brushing her cheek. "We haven't had a chance to talk alone since the rodeo."

What could it hurt if Riley relaxed in the hot tub and she sat in the chair? "Fine."

Flashing his trademark sexy grin he sauntered into the bathroom area. She wished the tub wasn't in the middle of the room but this was Vegas and everything sat out in the open. "Do you want me to close the curtains?"

"Leave them alone." He ran the water.

After she lowered the lights, Maria retreated to the window. Keeping her back to the tub, she watched tourists and gamblers stroll along the strip, ducking in and out of the casinos.

She kept her eyes on the activity outside the hotel but her sensitive ears caught the sound of rustling clothes as Riley stripped. The clank of his belt buckle against the tile floor startled her and she jumped inside her skin.

An image of a naked man appeared in the window glass. Maria blinked hard but couldn't make herself turn away. Riley was magnificent—tall, with lean muscles and six-pack abs. Her gaze skirted his loins, focusing on his legs. His thighs bunched with muscle when he raised his leg and stepped into the tub.

A guttural groan rumbled in his chest. Maria checked over her shoulder and witnessed the grimace on Riley's face as he sank into the water. Had he injured his back more seriously than he'd admitted? Maria retrieved the complimentary bath salts from the counter and dumped them into the hot water, careful to keep her eyes off his naked torso.

"You'll smell like a flower, but the Epsom salts will ease the soreness in your back," she said. Next, she grabbed a hand towel and folded it into a pillow. "Lift your head." He complied and she wedged the cotton between his neck and the tub.

Eyes closed, he muttered, "That feels great, thanks."

Maria gave into temptation and peered below the water level. Her breath caught at the sight of Riley's erection. It had been a long time since a man had made her perspire. Made her heart race. Her pulse pound. And the tiny little sparks that tickled her privates... She couldn't remember the last time she'd experienced those.

"I can explain." Riley grasped her hand, his wet fingers entwining with hers.

With her defenses weakening by the second, she decided to play dumb until she recovered her wits. "Explain what?"

"Whatever Amy told you earlier."

Maria had all evening to come to terms with the information she'd learned about Riley and Amy's relationship. She'd decided she was relieved Riley wasn't perfect—his infidelity made it easier to protect her heart from him.

"I don't want to waste time guessing what you ladies talked about, so you tell me," Riley said.

Most men would have evaded discussing a meeting between their ex and current...whatever she was to Riley. It didn't surprise her that he'd rather face the music than tiptoe around the three-thousand-pound elephant in the room. She, however, preferred to leave well enough alone.

"There's nothing to explain." At his startled expression, she added, "What happened between you and Amy stays between you and Amy."

Learning that Riley had cheated on his former girlfriend had turned out to be a good thing. Until today, Maria had believed Riley a saint—the only mark against him had been his age. Riley was a nice man with a good heart but now that she'd discovered he wasn't perfect she could lay to rest all her fairy-tale fantasies about a future with him.

No longer did it matter that she was ten years his senior. She didn't have to fret that Riley might want children one day and she didn't. What difference did it make that he came from a wealthy, privileged family and she resided in the inner city? None of it mattered, because she'd never marry a man who'd cheated. *Once a cheater always a cheater.*

After her experience with Fernando, Maria swore she'd never allow another man to hurt her that way again. There would be no guilty feelings for caving in to the desire that had built steadily between her and Riley these past weeks. She was free to be with him for however long their affair—if that's what he wanted with her—lasted. Afterward, she'd walk away with no regrets. No broken heart.

"Are you sure you don't have any questions about my relationship with Amy?"

Maria ignored the suspicious note in his voice and focused her energy on changing the mood. She sat on the edge of the tub and poured a dollop of body wash onto the loofah sponge. Unlike a lot of men the same age as Maria, Riley's body was in prime condition. She slid the sponge across his shoulder, then down his arm, rubbing the large bicep, before moving to his chest, specifically the small tuft of black hair between his pectoral muscles. When her fingernails grazed his skin, he closed his eyes and moaned. Feeling bolder, Maria washed Riley's belly, the action triggering a movement below the water surface. She dragged the sponge along his thigh, then reversed direction and caressed the inside of the leg, making sure she narrowly missed his erection.

Leaning over the tub she soaped his foot. Her bathrobe parted, exposing her breast, and Riley caressed her tight nipple with his wet fingers. An achy knot formed in Maria's stomach as she dropped the sponge into the water and drove Riley wild with her hand. He threaded his fingers through her hair, tugging her head closer until their lips touched. Slow and easy, he kissed her.

"Make love to me, Riley," Maria whispered.

"Are you sure?"

The only thing Maria was certain of was that she couldn't live with herself if she allowed this moment to slip away. "Very sure."

Riley sprang to a standing position, water sluicing down his body, leaving Maria eye-level with a part of his anatomy she very much wanted inside her. Slowly she stood, giving him room to step from the tub. "Leave the jets running," he said, then scooped her into his arms.

"Your back," she protested.

"Sweetheart, the only pain I feel right now is below the waist." He carried her to the bed then covered her body with his.

The flashing neon lights outside the window cast a magical glow over the room. Riley was the sexiest man Maria had ever laid eyes on and he was all hers. *For tonight.*

"Be sure about this." His gaze pinned her. "I don't want any regrets."

She pressed her finger to his lips. "You talk too

much." Hypnotized by his blue eyes, she lifted her head, closing the distance between their mouths. Her bathrobe landed on the floor and Maria resisted the urge to cover herself with the edge of the comforter. Good grief, she was a mature woman whose body reflected her age. She took solace in believing that if Riley wanted young and firm he'd be with a buckle bunny right now.

He kissed a path down the center of her chest and her back arched, begging for more. "Where did you get this scar?" Riley caressed the quarter-size circle of puckered flesh on the outside of her right thigh.

"You'll ruin the mood with questions," she said.

Concern darkened his eyes and a piece of Maria's heart tore off. "Tell me what happened," he demanded.

"A bullet grazed me."

"Who shot you?" He kissed her scar.

Evidently their lovemaking would go no further until Riley had the answers he sought. "It was an accident. A boy entered my class carrying a gun, saying he'd forgotten to leave it at home. I told him to put it on my desk and he did. Then I called school security to collect the weapon. They arrived and when I went to hand it to the officer, the gun discharged, hitting me in the leg."

"You were lucky you weren't injured worse."

"No, I'm lucky the bullet didn't hit the officer or one of my students." She tugged a strand of his hair. "Now can we get back to…"

Riley nibbled a path down her leg, ending at her foot, where he nuzzled the arch.

"Stop!" She giggled. "That tickles."

His mouth moved to her ankle, then along the inside of her leg, his hot breath heating her flesh. "Tell me if this tickles." The air whooshed from Maria's lungs at the intimate caress. No man had ever taken this much care to arouse her. Heat spread through her body, leaving her flushed and gasping for air…a few seconds later her soul shattered into a million bright pieces.

Riley rested on his elbows and stared.

"What?" she whispered.

He tugged a strand of damp hair stuck to her cheek and grinned. "You've been ridden hard and put up wet."

"That's because I'm in bed with a rodeo cowboy."

Capturing Maria's mouth, Riley kissed the sass out of her. Her body shuddered, reminding him of his own unfulfilled need. He fumbled with his wallet on the nightstand. "Fasten your seat belt, darlin'," he said, then took Maria on a ride with more hills and drops than the hotel roller coaster.

IN THE AFTERMATH OF THEIR lovemaking Riley tightened his arms around Maria and snuggled her to his side. The soft rumble of the hot-tub jets echoed through the room. Since he'd met Maria, Riley had fantasized about having sex with her. Maria's enthusiastic response had wowed him. Riley groaned when she slid her leg between his, rubbing her lush breasts against his side. All she had to do was inhale and his body was ready for her again.

"Have I told you how much I enjoy being with you?" he whispered in her ear. "You're a special woman. I admire what you're doing for the boys. How you try to protect others."

Her fingers inched their way down his chest and Riley grasped her wrist before she dipped beneath the bedsheet. "Wait." He shifted onto his side and faced her. That Maria appeared reluctant to discuss his past relationship with Amy troubled Riley. He wanted the truth out in the open so they could deal with it. "I'm not making excuses for myself, but—"

"What you did in the past doesn't matter."

If Maria cared the least bit for him, then his cheating on Amy should damn well matter.

"We're having fun together, Riley. Let's live in the moment. No worries about the past. Or the future."

Feeling as if he'd been blindsided, Riley's stomach clenched and he closed his eyes against the pain. He'd finally realized his dream of coaxing Maria into his bed only to discover she was with him for all the wrong reasons.

Maria threaded her fingers through his hair and nudged his mouth toward hers. "Kiss me."

Frustration fueled the urgency behind Riley's kiss. He tried to convey without words that what they'd shared hadn't been a *good time* for him. Maria was the first woman he'd ever envisioned standing at his side a year from now. Ten years from now. Forever from now.

A fist banged against the connecting door between the boys' and Maria's room, abruptly ending their kiss.

"Yeah?" Riley called out.

"Can we watch another pay-per-view movie?" Alonso's voice filtered through the wall.

"Go ahead."

"When you comin' back?" Victor joined the conversation.

"After I discuss tomorrow's schedule with Ms. Alvarez."

"Yeah, sure." Snickers followed Victor's comment. The mood broken, Riley left the bed.

After Riley retreated to the bathroom, Maria decided she was one fortunate lady. Stretching her arms above her head, she arched her back, relishing the twinges and tiny aches in her muscles. When she opened her eyes, Riley stood at the end of the bed.

"You're a beautiful woman, Maria."

No. She wasn't beautiful. Attractive maybe. But for now...tonight...she wouldn't deny his charge. "You'd better leave before they suspect..."

"They suspect." He winked. "But I'm not one of those guys who brags about his conquests." He shut off the hot-tub jets, then walked to the other side of the bed and retrieved Maria's robe from the floor.

"What about your back? Will you be able to ride tomorrow?" She slipped on the robe.

"I'll soak in the hot tub beforehand." He stuffed his shirt into his jeans and zipped his pants. "How about letting the boys sleep in and you and I eat breakfast together in the morning?"

"I'd love that."

He kissed her cheek, then her mouth—slow, hot and deep. "Be ready by seven," he whispered.

The quiet click of the door echoed through the room. Grateful for time alone, Maria studied her reflection in the mirror against the wall. She touched her fingertips to her swollen lips. Surely the boys didn't believe she and Riley had...had...

Made love.

There. She'd said it. What she and Riley had shared was more than sex. When Riley had held her in his arms, Maria had forgotten how wrong they were for each other. It would be so easy to lose her heart to Riley. He made her feel young and desirable and he restored her faith in the goodness of people. Riley made each day something to cherish—not just to survive. Though she was tempted to throw caution to the wind and allow herself to be in a committed relationship with Riley, she couldn't trust him not to stray once the newness of their lovemaking wore off. Better for both of them if they kept things light. Easy. Uncomplicated.

What happens in Vegas stays in Vegas.

As long as Maria remembered that, she couldn't get hurt.

RILEY ENTERED THE ROOM THE boys shared and three sets of smirking eyes greeted him.

"We heard you guys," Victor said, cracking a smile.

No, they didn't—not with the hot-tub jets running while he and Maria had made love.

"Be careful not to malign your teacher." Riley scowled at the boys.

"What's malign?" Victor asked.

"It means you shouldn't criticize Ms. Alvarez in a mean or hurtful way," Alonso said.

"I meant—"

"Nothing," Riley interrupted Victor. The teens backed off and he asked, "What movie are you watching?"

"A thriller about a man-eating python," Cruz said.

Too agitated to retreat to his room, Riley stretched out on one of the beds and groaned when a sharp twinge zapped his lower back.

"Did you get hurt today?" Cruz sat on the end of the bed.

"Pulled a few muscles."

"Do you get hurt a lot?"

"Not as much as other cowboys."

"How come you keep ridin' then?"

"I entered a junior rodeo on a dare when I was in tenth grade," Riley said. His father had been nagging Riley to take on more responsibility in the horse barns—the last place he'd wanted to spend time. Instead, he'd snuck off with his friends to a local rodeo.

"What happened?" Cruz asked.

"I won."

"So that's why you kept rodeoing?"

"No. I discovered that I craved the adrenaline rush I got from trying to tame a wild bronc." And rodeo had angered his father. What teen didn't find satisfaction in pissing off a parent?

"I get the same high when I break the law," Cruz said.

The more Riley learned about Cruz the more he believed rodeo might be the ticket to prevent the teen from following in his father's footsteps. Cruz lived in a world of gangs, violence and crime—it was all he knew. Riley bet the kid wouldn't be able to turn his back on that way of life without suffering withdrawal symptoms. "You'd be good at rodeo. But there's a price to pay if you get hurt."

"Do you know if my dad got hurt a lot?"

"I don't. You'll have to ask him when you see him on Sunday."

"What are you talking about?"

"Didn't Ms. Alvarez tell you?"

"Tell me what?"

Shoot. Riley should have confirmed the visit with Maria before they'd left Albuquerque, but he'd expected she'd have told him if the prison had denied Cruz a visit with his father. "After the rodeo on Sunday, we're flying to Sioux Falls. Ms. Alvarez arranged for you to see your dad."

"You're not joking, are you?"

"Nope. Barring any bad weather, we should arrive at the prison around six o'clock in the evening."

"Thanks," Cruz said.

"Don't thank me. Thank Ms. Alvarez." With the muted sounds of screaming python victims ringing in his ear, Riley closed his eyes and willed his mind to empty of all thoughts but making love to Maria.

Wow. Double wow. He'd fantasized about having sex with her since the day he'd landed his plane in the salvage yard. His fantasies hadn't compared to the real thing.

He could feel the softness of her skin rubbing against his. Her fingers tickling his thigh. Her nails biting into his flesh. He'd won his first go-round today but he hadn't won Maria. Riley worried over her easy acceptance of their lovemaking. She'd made it clear she was in it for the sex—a wild weekend in Vegas.

This trip was supposed to have been his chance to prove to Maria that there was more between them than sexual attraction. Instead, she'd given him the impression that she wasn't interested in a deeper, more meaningful relationship. Tomorrow was another chance to prove to Maria that what they'd shared tonight was more than just a wild ride.

Chapter Eleven

"Ladies and gents, this is the final day of the Hell-dorado Rodeo competition here in lucky Las Vegas!"

Maria scanned the crowd but saw no sign of Amy in the stands. Thank goodness. Even though she'd told Riley his relationship with his ex-girlfriend wasn't a big deal…it was. Maria had difficulty reconciling the cheating Riley with the Riley who'd offered to introduce the boys to his competitors hanging out in the cowboy-ready area. Part of her wished she'd never run into Amy, but then she'd have never learned that Riley wasn't as perfect as she'd made him out to be. In a weird way the knowledge of Riley's past infidelities had both protected and wounded Maria's heart.

The brief time she'd spent in Riley's arms proved how vulnerable she was to the cowboy. The knowledge of why Amy had ended her relationship with Riley had done little to subdue Maria's craving to make love with him. No man had ever made her feel so special and desirable. As long as she kept her feelings for Riley in check and understood that their relationship could go no farther than the bedroom, she wouldn't get hurt.

For a mature woman who'd witnessed events in real life that most people only watched in TV dramas,

Maria was embarrassingly gullible. Older didn't mean wiser. Even though Riley acted mature for his age he was young and entitled to his share of mistakes as he matured. She'd certainly made a few blunders in her twenties.

"Folks, today's pot is worth ten thousand dollars to the cowboy or cowgirl who walks away with first place in their event." The young woman crowned Miss Helldorado paraded a trophy in front of the cheering fans.

Ten thousand was a fortune to Maria—pocket change to a man who flew his own plane. This morning Riley had told her over breakfast that a win today would put him in the running for a trip back to Vegas in December. He'd also said he planned to compete in as many rodeos as possible to prepare for the finals.

December was three months away. A lot could happen between now and then. Even so, Maria fantasized about spending Christmas with Riley. The holiday hadn't been the same since her brother had passed away. Maria had stopped stringing lights up and decorating the artificial tree when her mother had complained that the traditions made her more heartbroken over the death of her son.

The shrill blast of trumpets cleared the gloomy memories from Maria's head. A horse-drawn buckboard, carrying the rodeo sponsors to the VIP seating area, entered the arena. While the announcer introduced the men and women, Maria watched Riley and the boys.

Cruz had been especially thrilled when Riley suggested the teens witness today's competitions from behind the chutes. Maria noted a change in Cruz's demeanor this weekend. An aura of new energy surrounded him. Two weeks from now Cruz turned eighteen and Maria hoped he'd continue to pursue his GED and not drop out of her class. With any luck, a visit with his father in jail would convince Cruz to stick to his goals.

"Folks, it's time to kick off the saddle-bronc competition!" Once the cheers died down, the announcer continued. "Gate two's where all the action is. Ed Parker from Albuquerque, New Mexico, is comin' out on Stingray. Parker hasn't had a top-five finish in two years. He's currently in sixth place. Let's see if the next eight seconds changes his luck!"

Stingray bolted from the chute, bucked twice then reared. Maria prayed Gil Parker's son would keep his seat. Stingray established a pattern of bucking twice, then spinning to the right. A half second before the buzzer sounded, Ed sailed over the bronc's head. The pickup men moved in and guided the horse out of the arena.

"Maybe next time, cowboy!"

Five more riders came and went—two managing to remain in the saddle until the buzzer. "Eighty-three is the score to beat and we got two cowboys left who are gonna give it try!" The announcer spoke over the crowd's applause. "Nick Bass, from Sierra Vista, Arizona, is new to the circuit. You might remember his earlier performance. He came in one point shy of Riley Fitzgerald. He needs a good ride if he intends to upset the reigning world champion."

Once the noise level dropped a notch the announcer said, "The action's at gate five! Bass is gonna strut his stuff on Holly Jolly."

Holly Jolly was an appropriate name for the bronc that jumped out of the chute. All four legs left the ground when the horse performed an equestrian happy dance. After a few seconds, the bronc ran out of jollies and its bucking dwindled to a few kicks. Bass kept his seat until the buzzer then dismounted. Holly Jolly trotted out of the arena on his own.

"Bass made it to eight, folks. Let's see what the judges think of Holly Jolly's performance."

The Jumbotron above the VIP seats displayed an 84.

"Fitzgerald could be our winner today if he keeps his seat on Tranquility!" More applause. "Don't let the horse's name fool you none. Tranquility is notorious for brewin' up a storm!"

The crowd stomped their feet on the metal bleachers. "Let's see if Fitzgerald and Tranquility can get the job done. Gate seven!"

Riley climbed the chute rails. Cruz, Victor and Alonso perched on the top rung to watch the action. Riley didn't waste any time preparing for his ride. A few seconds after he settled into the saddle and wrapped the rein around his hand, the gate opened and Tranquility burst into the arena.

The bronc twisted to the left then reared before slamming back to the ground and spinning right. In a succession of spins and bucks, Tranquility edged closer to the rails. A collective gasp echoed through the stands when the bronc hit the gate. From that moment on, the action in the arena played out in slow motion before Maria's eyes. The boys jumping off the rails... Riley's leg slamming into the chute door... The grimace on Riley's face...

The buzzer sounded but Riley held on through a second round of bucking as the pickup men attempted to corner Tranquility. Riley released the rein and jumped to the ground. He stumbled once, twice, then unable to maintain his balance, he slid face-first into the dirt. The pickup men guided the bronc out of the arena and Riley slowly got to his knees.

"Well, folks, what'd I say about Tranquility? That horse is a cyclone on four hooves!"

Maria pressed her fingers to her mouth as she watched Riley struggle to his feet then limp from the arena.

"Fitzgerald's gonna be okay, folks!" The crowd applauded.

The Jumbotron flashed a score of 85. "Fitzgerald takes first place, which puts him back in the race for a national title!"

"Excuse me. Pardon me." Maria made her way out of the stands then hurried to find Riley and the boys. When she arrived behind the chutes, Riley was surrounded by cowboys. She squeezed into the circle and clutched his shirtsleeve. "Are you okay?"

"I'm good as gold, darlin'."

The crowd snickered, but Maria failed to find humor in his remark. Riley had scared ten years off her life in a little over eight seconds. Reporters were eager for a word with him so she stepped aside. Cruz remained next to Riley listening to the reporter's questions and Riley's responses. Victor and Alonso had lost interest in the commotion and walked off to watch rodeo workers load a bull into a chute. After ten minutes of nonstop questions and autograph signing, Riley glanced her way. His gentle smile tugged at her heartstrings. He thanked reporters, then excused himself and limped to her side.

"I won."

Despite her concern she laughed at his arrogance. "I

know. Congratulations. That was an impressive ride. Did you hurt your leg?"

"A bruise. Ready to head to the airport? Cruz is eager to see his dad."

"I'm not so sure about that." Maria pointed to the teen, who was conversing with a blond buckle bunny. As much as Maria had enjoyed the weekend in Vegas, it was time to leave Sin City behind. She signaled to Victor and Alonso and the boys caught Cruz's attention. After Riley collected his winning check, they piled into a cab and swung by the hotel, where a bellman loaded their luggage into the trunk and wished them a safe flight.

When they arrived at the airstrip, Maria pulled Riley aside. "Are you certain you're able to fly with a sore leg?"

"You worry too much." He brushed a strand of hair from her cheek, then limped off to file a flight plan.

Maria wished she possessed his positive view of life. Even if she was able to forget his cheating on Amy, Maria's pessimistic view of the world would drag Riley down and eventually he'd realize that she was a dark cloud hanging over his head and not the ray of sunshine he'd first believed.

THE SOUTH DAKOTA STATE Penitentiary in Sioux Falls was nothing to write home and brag about. Cruz fidgeted as they stood outside the facility, waiting for Maria to confirm the teen's visit with his father. The kid was nervous. Who wouldn't be, seeing their father behind bars? Victor and Alonso sensed their friend's unease and hovered by his side, offering silent support.

After five minutes, Maria signaled them to follow her. Except for the female prison guard behind the registration window the visitor's welcome room was empty.

"Cruz, it will be about thirty minutes before they bring your father down." Maria squeezed the teen's arm reassuringly and smiled. "The officer needs you to go with her."

"Why?" Cruz's gaze darted between Maria and Riley.

"They need to screen you for weapons or contraband," Riley said.

"Can we go with him?" Victor asked.

"Cruz is the only one approved for a visit," Maria said. She coaxed the teen to the window, where he answered questions then followed the guard out of the room.

"Look, Alonso. The prisoners are outside." Victor stood before a large tinted window facing the grounds. A sign on the wall assured visitors that prisoners could not see through the glass into the waiting room.

Riley joined the boys at the window. The inmates broke into teams—a few played basketball while others lifted weights or talked and smoked in small groups.

"Look at that tattoo." Victor pointed to a man hovering near the window. "That's the symbol of the Aryan Brotherhood." Right then the convict faced the window and sneered, revealing several missing teeth. Alonso and Victor jumped back and the man laughed as if he knew he was being watched.

"I feel sorry for Cruz's dad," Alonso whispered.

"More incentive to work hard for Ms. Alvarez and earn a GED," Riley said.

Victor grimaced. "What good's a GED if I don't know what I wanna do with my life?" Right then the teen's cell phone bleeped and Victor stepped outside to talk.

Riley lost himself in thought. Shoot, he didn't know what he wanted to do with his life, either; but after making love to Maria he believed it was imperative that he get his act together and make a decision about his future. He couldn't continue to rodeo and rely on his trust fund to pay his way through life.

He believed Maria didn't begrudge him for his privileged upbringing—she wasn't that kind of woman. But the man she gave her heart to and wanted to spend the rest of her years with would be a man who blazed his own trail. If he wanted to be with Maria he needed a game plan for his future—one that included her.

"Everything okay?" Maria stopped by his side.

Riley slung an arm around her shoulders but she moved away, breaking contact. Was she worried the boys would guess they were more than friends or was her lukewarm response a signal that what they'd shared in Vegas had ended when they'd left the city? This wasn't the place or time to discuss their relationship, but before the day was through Riley intended to have a heart-to-heart with Maria.

"Where did Victor go?" Maria glanced around the room.

"He's out front talking on his phone."

Once outside Maria froze when she heard the words Los Locos come out of Victor's mouth.

"Yeah, man, tell the homies I'm in. No, man, I'm for real." Victor kept his back to Maria and continued talking. "I gotta stay a few more weeks at that stupid ranch then I'm comin' back to the 'hood."

Maria's heart sank. Since when had Victor changed his mind about liking it at Gateway Ranch?

"Yeah, I could be a lookout for the gang. Just give me a chance." Victor glanced over his shoulder, his face paling when he saw Maria. "Later, homie." He ended the call.

"Are you running with the Los Locos, Victor?" She engaged the boy in a stare-down.

"What if I am?" The teen jutted his chin.

From the bits and pieces of conversation she'd over-heard, Maria guessed that Victor hadn't yet been ac-cepted into the gang but it was only a matter of time before he ran with the hoodlums.

"What about your GED? Are you going to throw all that studying away?"

"No. I'm gonna take the tests, but—"

"But what, Victor?"

"But I'm not Cruz. I don't wanna bust broncs. And I'm not Alonso. I don't wanna go to college." He scuffed the toe of his shoe against the cement. "I can make a lot of money in the gang."

"Why all of a sudden are you worried about making money?"

"I wanna be like Riley. The dude walks around with hundred-dollar bills in his wallet. He stays in fancy hotel suites in Vegas and flies his own plane."

"Then go to college and earn a degree, get a good job and save your money."

"Riley didn't get his money from no college degree. He said his grandpa left him a bank account." Victor's eyes narrowed. "I don't have a grandpa who's gonna leave me millions of dollars. But I can buy stuff and get me a bunch of those Benjamins if I hang with the Los Locos."

"You believe becoming a member of a gang is the fast track to fame and fortune?"

"It's the only track in the 'hood, Ms. Alvarez. As soon as I save enough money I'll quit the gang and move away from the 'hood and get a real job."

They both knew once Victor joined the Los Locos he'd never leave the gang or the 'hood alive. Maria's father had been right—Riley wasn't a good role model for the teens. Cruz, Alonso and Victor weren't mature enough to understand that not everyone in life received a free ride. That the majority of the people on earth had to *work* for the things they desired.

"Promise me one thing, Victor."

"What?"

"You won't have any more contact with the Los Locos until you earn your GED and leave the ranch."

"But—"

"No calls. No texts. Nothing." If Maria believed it would prevent Victor from contacting the gang she'd confiscate his phone. But if the teen was determined to stay in touch with the Los Locos there was little she could do to stop him. "If you can't keep that promise then you pack your bags and leave the ranch when we return tonight." She was relying on Victor's friendship with Cruz and Alonso to keep him at the ranch until she found a way to deter him from joining the gang.

"Everything okay out here?" Riley poked his head outside the building.

"We're fine," Maria said.

Victor shoved his phone into his pocket. "Is Cruz back?" he asked.

"Yep. We're ready to leave." Cruz and Alonso pushed past Riley out of the building. The stony expression on Cruz's face gave no indication how the visit with his father had gone. A moment later the same cab and driver that had dropped them off at the prison arrived and they headed to the airstrip in silence.

After Riley filed another flight plan, Cruz asked Maria if he could switch places with her and keep Riley company in the cockpit. Thirty minutes later the *Dark Stranger* was airborne. Once the plane reached cruising altitude, Riley leveled off.

"My dad's heard of you."

"Yeah?" Riley didn't know how unless the man had caught a televised rodeo on TV.

"He wanted to know why I was hanging around with a rich cowboy."

"What'd you tell him?"

"I told him about Ms. Alvarez and how I got kicked out of school and she was helping me get a GED and you got us a place to stay at the ranch where you were teaching me about rodeo."

"What'd he say?"

"That I should find a better teacher."

"Did he mean me or Ms. Alvarez?"

"You."

Go figure. "Did your dad recommend anyone in particular?"

"Yeah, a dude named Drew Rawlins."

Riley's ghostly nemesis.

"My dad said Rawlins is really tough."

"Rawlins was good but he struggled with injuries and had to retire."

Riley doubted he'd ever earn the respect he deserved unless he won the NFR outright this December. One thing for sure, he wouldn't win if he didn't focus on rodeo. He needed to keep his priorities straight or he'd lose his chance to prove he was the best in the world at bustin' broncs.

"My dad said rich people don't know how to fight for what they want 'cause they never had to go without."

Riley's father had warned him others would believe as much and that he'd have to work twice as hard to earn respect. Case in point—Maria. He had to find a way to prove to her he was more than a good time or temporary amusement. "A bronc can't tell a rich cowboy from a poor one nor does he care." Irritated, he changed the subject. "Did you and your dad talk about anything else?"

"He asked about my mom. I told him the truth. That she gets high all the time."

Riley remained quiet and waited for Cruz to volunteer more information.

"No one told him my brother was dead," Cruz whispered.

"Your father must have been pretty upset."

"He told me no matter how long it takes, I should stay in Ms. Alvarez's class and get my GED."

"Good advice."

After a short silence, Cruz added, "My dad didn't mean to kill that man."

"I'm sure he didn't." But T.C. *had* killed a man and now he had to pay a hefty price.

"He doesn't want me to end up in the slammer like him."

"Most fathers want their kids to turn out better."

"Yeah, I guess."

"Did your dad say what he does to keep busy?"

"He's got a job in the prison factory making commercial draperies." Cruz glanced at Riley. "Does that mean he sews stuff?"

"Probably."

"That sucks."

It sure does.

"He said to thank you for bringing me to visit."

"Ms. Alvarez should get his thanks. She's the one who arranged the meeting."

Riley spent the next few minutes communicating with Blue Skies Regional Airport. After he'd been cleared for landing, he said, "There's a junior rodeo in El Paso at the end of October."

"That's two months away."

Not quite. "Seven weeks. Think you can pass your GED exams by then?"

"Yeah. But I'd need a saddle."

"I'll buy you one before I leave."

"I thought I had to earn—"

"Consider the equipment a loan." The kid couldn't very well learn how to rodeo without gear. "If you don't earn your GED, the gear's mine."

"You gonna be around to help me?"

"I've got a string of rodeos to get in before the finals in December, but I'll squeeze in a few lessons before the El Paso rodeo." Riley turned the plane eastward. "And I'll make sure the other cowboys at the ranch help you."

"What about you and Ms. Alvarez?"

"What about us?"

"Aren't you guys…you know, doin' it?"

"Ms. Alvarez and I are good friends."

Cruz frowned. "I thought you and her…you know?"

"You leave Ms. Alvarez and me to our own business. Okay?"

"Just sayin', man." The teen listened to his iPod the remainder of the flight. When Riley landed the plane at the airport, Maria's father waited inside the hangar.

"You did a fantastic job on the repairs," Riley praised Ricardo.

"Are we going back to the ranch?" As soon as Alonso asked the question, Maria's father excused himself and retreated to his office—obviously the older man was uncomfortable around the teens. "Load your bags into the truck. I'll be right there."

Once the teens left the hangar, Maria spoke. "Thank you for making this weekend special for the boys."

What about you? Had Maria's time in Vegas been special? "I wish you could come on the road with me but you'd be a major distraction." He leaned in to kiss her cheek but she dodged the caress. He was batting oh for two so far today. "Cruz wants to compete in the junior rodeo at the end of October. I told him to keep studying and that I'd try to return to the ranch between now and then to give him a few lessons."

"That's not a good idea."

"What do you mean?" Riley's gut clenched when Maria refused to make eye contact.

"It's best if you keep your distance from the boys."

He opened his mouth but shock barred the words from escaping.

"I appreciate everything you've done, but—"

"Stop." Riley shoved his fingers through his hair. "Did the guys tease you about us sleeping together in Vegas?"

Maria glanced over her shoulder to check on her father but he'd disappeared inside the office. "This has nothing to do with us. I caught Victor on his cell phone talking to a member of the Los Locos gang."

"What does that have to do with me?"

"Victor believes joining a gang is a shortcut to making a lot of money."

"He should know better than that. You have to work hard if you expect to own the finer things in life."

"I agree, Riley, but Victor sees you throwing your money around, paying for fancy hotels in Vegas, flying your own airplane...don't you understand? He wants to live your life, only he doesn't have a wealthy grandfather. The only way he believes he can make a lot of money is by joining a gang."

"I'll have a talk with Victor and—"

"It would be best if you stayed away from the boys."

Frustrated, Riley clenched his hands into fists. "And do you believe I should keep my distance from you, too?"

"Yes."

The whispered word sliced Riley's heart in two. "Then it's a good thing I'm on the road until the middle of October." Maybe it was wishful thinking or a trick of the lighting, but he swore Maria's eyes shone with tears. He wanted to ask if she regretted making love with him but didn't have the guts. He prayed Maria's heart would grow fonder of him over the next several weeks. "Walk me to my truck?" He didn't want to leave without kissing her.

"Sure." They stepped into the shadows outside the hangar and Riley slowed his steps. "This weekend meant a lot to me." When Maria remained silent, he pulled her close. "I care about you, Maria. More than I've cared about any woman. Don't quit me."

"We'd be dragging out a relationship that has nowhere to go and—"

"If this is about Amy, I—"

"What happened between you and Amy doesn't matter, because we can't be together." Maria's smile wobbled. "Fly safe, Riley."

Damn, this was not the memory he wanted to take with him after a great weekend in Vegas. Maria might believe she'd gotten the final word in, but, as far as Riley was concerned, they were far from finished. He kissed her, pouring his emotions into the embrace, showing her how much he wanted her…heart, soul and body.

Then he left her gasping for breath and walked away.

Chapter Twelve

Six weeks.

Six long weeks had passed since Riley left Albuquerque and hit the rodeo circuit.

Late Friday afternoon Maria stood outside the corral at the Gateway Ranch, watching Cruz practice his rodeo skills on a horse named Skippy. She shivered as the brisk October breeze whipped her hair about her head. She'd arrived late to tutor the boys, because Judge Hamel had requested a meeting with her to discuss Cruz's progress. Cruz had fulfilled his hundred hours of community service, but both she and the judge agreed that it was in the teen's best interest to remain at the ranch until he completed the requirements to earn his GED. One test remained—math. Not Cruz's strong subject.

Since the rodeo in Vegas, time had crawled to a standstill for Maria. No matter how busy she kept herself, every other thought centered on Riley. Her feelings for the cowboy were a tangled mess, and she missed him. Missed his smile. His grin. The way he goofed off and made the boys laugh.

"Cruz looks as if he'll be ready for his first junior

rodeo at the end of the month," Gil Parker said when he stopped at Maria's side.

"He's getting better, isn't he?" Maria was impressed with the way Cruz listened to the ranch hand giving him pointers.

"Riley phoned an hour ago. He should be here by supper time."

Maria's heartbeat jumped out of sync for several seconds before returning to a normal rhythm. "Has he been winning?"

Gil frowned. "I thought you two were—" He cleared his throat. "I'd presumed he'd been calling you with updates."

"I've been busy with my students." She'd listened to Riley's first voice mail message weeks ago. He'd pleaded for a chance to make things right with Victor and with her. Tears had filled her eyes and from that day forward she'd deleted his messages without listening to them. One of them had to be the adult. Since she was older...

"Spoke to my son Ed last night. He said Riley moved into the top ten. He's taken first or second place in every rodeo since his big win in Las Vegas. Billy Stover beat him out in Phoenix two weeks ago, but Ed claims Riley drew a lazy bronc in that go-round."

"I'm glad he's doing well." That Riley was winning again proved he hadn't lied to Maria when he'd insisted she was a distraction. She hadn't wanted to believe she interfered with his concentration, because then she couldn't dismiss Riley's feelings for her as those of a young man with his first crush on an older woman.

Gil tipped his hat toward Cruz. "How's he doing with his schoolwork?"

"He'll be ready to take his final test next week."

"Think he'll pass?"

"I hope so." Victor and Alonso had completed their exams and earned their GEDs two weeks ago. Gil had offered to pay the two teens for their work if they decided to remain at the ranch while Cruz studied. Alonso jumped at the opportunity but convincing Victor to remain hadn't been easy when he was eager to join the Los Locos gang. In the end Cruz and Alonso had been the ones to talk him into staying.

"What you're doing for the boys..." Maria blinked back tears. "Thank you for opening your heart and this ranch to them."

Gil smiled. "Everyone deserves a second chance."

As much as they might want to, the boys couldn't live at the ranch forever; and Maria worried that if she didn't persuade Victor to walk away from the Los Locos he'd be lost to her forever.

"Here he goes." Gil pointed to Cruz.

Shouts of encouragement erupted from the cowhands when Cruz settled onto the back of the bronc. Pride filled her as she watched her student cling to the saddle. The horse didn't buck as violently as the animals in the Vegas rodeo, but the bronc had plenty of spunk for a beginner. Cruz slid sideways but managed to remain in the saddle. Eight seconds passed and Alonso clanged a cow bell. Several cowboys leapt into the pen ready to intervene should Cruz need help.

The teen swung his leg over the saddle and launched himself into the air. He landed on both feet, but the impact sent him sprawling forward and he slid on his belly.

"Dismount needs a little work, Cruz!"

Maria whirled at the familiar voice. Riley strolled

toward the corral, his sexy swagger and engaging smile sending a tiny thrill through her. She waited for him to notice her but he focused on the action inside the pen.

"I made it to eight, Riley!" Cruz spit dirt from his mouth.

"I saw. Good job!" Riley stopped near Gil and the men shook hands.

"Didn't expect you for another hour or two," Gil said.

"Caught a tailwind." Riley spared Maria a quick glance. "Hello, Maria."

Hurt by the tepid greeting, she responded in kind. "Riley." What had she expected after she'd ignored his phone calls and text messages?

"Heard you set fire to the rodeo circuit these past few weeks," Gil said.

"I had a good run."

"Look forward to hearing about your rides. See you folks at supper." Gil walked off.

Aside from the nick on his chin and a bruise on his right cheekbone Riley appeared in good shape. Maria never got the chance to ask how Riley's leg was healing before Cruz demanded his attention.

"Hey, Riley!" Cruz ducked between the slats of the pen. "Did you win a lot of rodeos?"

Alonso and Victor joined Cruz, peppering Riley with questions. Forgotten for the moment, Maria waited for a pause in conversation, then said, "Don't forget to tell Riley your good news."

"We passed our tests and got our GEDs," Alonso said.

"Alonso scored higher than me, but I still passed." Victor fist-pumped the air.

"That's great, guys. I'm proud of you," Riley said. "What about you, Cruz?"

"I have to take the math test."

"Math is tough, but I'm sure you're working hard with Ms. Alvarez on mastering the subject."

"Victor and Alonso have been quizzing Cruz to help prepare him for the test next week," Maria said.

"You'd better pass, Cruz. I paid your entry fee into the El Paso junior rodeo at the end of the month."

Maria squelched her anger at Riley's announcement. Was he purposefully going against her wishes that he keep his distance from the boys?

"Oh, man, really?" Cruz's eyes lit with excitement.

"Can me and Victor go, too?" Alonso asked.

"As long as Cruz passes his math exam, I'll fly all of you, including Ms. Alvarez, to El Paso."

"You gotta pass, Cruz," Alonso said.

Victor didn't appear as eager to watch Cruz compete as Alonso. Maria suspected he'd rather return to the 'hood. As much as she believed Riley's jet-setting lifestyle and big spending was responsible for Victor's desire to join the Los Locos, attending the rodeo in El Paso would keep the teen away from the gangbangers a while longer.

A ranch hand shouted for help stowing the rodeo gear and the boys took off at a sprint.

"That's an improvement." Riley watched the teens haul the equipment into the barn.

"Gil Parker is a saint in my book," Maria said. "Such a shame there aren't more people willing to offer at-risk teens a safe place to live, work and study their way to a better life."

Riley's expression sobered. "You didn't return my calls."

"I didn't see the point."

"We were friends before we slept together, weren't we?"

Maria glanced around, making sure no one eavesdropped on their conversation. "I did a lot of thinking while you were away." A little bit of crying, too. "Riley—"

"I want you to meet my parents, Maria."

What?

"My father's trying to close a deal with a former PRCA steer-wrestling champion and he needs me to schmooze the guy. My mother invited Peter Westin for dinner tomorrow night and I agreed to fly home for it."

"Riley, I don't see the purpose of meeting your parents when we're—"

"Friends?"

"Right."

"I can't think of a better reason than being friends to introduce you to my family."

Although Maria had decided that allowing her relationship with Riley to progress further was out of the question, a part of her wanted to see the place where he'd been raised—the environment and people who had molded him into the man he was today. A visit to Riley's childhood home would strengthen her memories of him—and memories were all she'd have once they parted ways. Even so, common sense insisted she offer a token protest. "I'm sure your mother wouldn't approve of you bringing home an older—"

"Please, Maria."

After all he'd done for the boys, Maria couldn't refuse him. "All right. I'll go."

"Good. Meet me at the airport tomorrow morning at ten."

"I have to work on Monday."

"We'll return Sunday."

"Casual or formal?"

"Formal."

Maria hoped the one and only cocktail dress she owned fit her. The last time she'd worn it she'd attended a co-worker's retirement party two years ago. She studied Riley's retreating backside as he headed for the barn. All these weeks she'd agonized over how she'd set Riley straight about their relationship only to learn he'd already decided they were better off being friends not lovers.

Maria didn't know if she was relieved or hurt that Riley had accepted defeat without a fight.

RILEY WATCHED MARIA OUT OF the corner of his eye as he drove twenty miles south of Lexington along the road bordering Belle Farms. Maria stared out the passenger window of the Lincoln Town Car, which had been dropped off for them at the estate's private airstrip. Maria's silence worried Riley. Hell, he'd been a mental mess since the rodeo in Las Vegas.

Maria was the first woman Riley had ever been serious about—really serious. When she hadn't returned his phone messages he'd deduced that she was intent on ending their relationship. The thought scared and angered him and he'd channeled that raw emotion into rodeo. The broncs hadn't stood a chance against Riley's bottled-up orneriness.

His goal had been to return to Albuquerque and pretend Maria hadn't ignored his calls, but he'd lost his courage and confronted her. As he'd predicted, Maria appeared intent on keeping that distance between them.

In a panic he'd invited her to Belle Farms, hoping to prove his feelings for her were honest and sincere. "The entrance is right here," he said, breaking the silence. He drove the Lincoln beneath the arching stone pillars and down the tree-lined drive. Maria's eyes widened—a common reaction by first-time visitors.

Albuquerque was unique in its own way, but the desert's brown-and-red clay colors paled in comparison to Kentucky's rich verdant pastureland, freshly whitewashed fencing and hunter-green horse barns. The road circled around a profusion of blooming rosebushes in front of a life-sized sculpture of a racing horse. He parked the Lincoln in front of the main house.

"It's beautiful," Maria whispered. Six massive pillars supported the overhang protecting the porch. A set of rocking chairs sat on both sides of the front door and large hanging baskets of red and yellow flowers added a splash of color to the home.

"My great-great-grandfather completed most of the renovations during his lifetime."

"It's remarkable and I haven't even seen the inside," Maria said.

He got out of the car, rounded the hood and held the door open for her.

"What about our bags?" she asked.

"I'll fetch them later." Halfway up the steps, the front door opened.

"Hey, Eunice." Riley greeted the housekeeper with a big hug. "I've brought a friend home to visit. Maria Alvarez, this is Belle Farms' housekeeper, Eunice Mays. She's been with the Fitzgerald family since before I was born."

The older woman with striking white hair hugged

Maria, squeezing the air from her lungs. "Welcome to Belle Farms, Miss Maria."

"Thank you, Eunice. It's a pleasure to meet you."

The housekeeper waved them into the foyer. "There's fresh-squeezed lemonade in the fridge."

Maria's feet remained rooted to the marble floor as she took inventory of the opulence surrounding her. Matching red velvet drapes with gold fringe adorned the floor-to-ceiling windows in the living room to her right and the dining room to her left. Mahogany bookcases lined the walls at the far end of the living room, where an antique desk sat. Maria guessed the piece of furniture was a family heirloom that had made the trip across the Atlantic. Persian rugs adorned dark wood floors, which gleamed in the sunlight pouring through the windows. Portraits of Fitzgerald ancestors hung on the foyer walls and along the staircase leading to a second-floor landing.

"Quit gawking at all the old stuff and come along, Miss Maria," the housekeeper said.

"Eunice hates antiques," Riley whispered. "She thinks the house is a museum."

"I heard that, young man."

The kitchen was a bit more modern—all the usual appliances. The double-wide refrigerator was built into the wall and a huge marble island sat in the middle of the room.

"You know what I think, Eunice? You hate being older than half the furnishings in this house," Riley teased.

The housekeeper smacked Riley across the shoulder. "Sit down before I send you to the corner."

Maria joined Riley at the island. "The corner? What's that?" she asked.

After setting a plate of cookies on the counter, Eunice retrieved a pitcher of lemonade from the refrigerator. "When Riley was naughty his mama would make him sit on a stool over there." Eunice pointed next to the back door.

"I hated that corner," Riley said. "Every time the door opened I got smacked."

Eunice laughed and the tension that had built in Maria since leaving Albuquerque eased. She hoped Riley's parents were as friendly and welcoming as the family housekeeper.

"Most of the time Eunice came to my rescue and convinced my mother to shorten the punishment time."

What an amazing childhood Riley must have experienced in the lap of luxury surrounded by love. No wonder he only saw the good in people.

"Is Bree out in the barn?" Riley asked.

"Where else would that girl be?" Eunice scoffed. "Your mama's in town talking to the caterers for tonight's dinner."

"Mom's not cooking?" Riley said.

"She took a tumble off her horse last week and sprained her wrist."

"She's okay otherwise?" Riley asked.

"Your mama's fine. But until she can cook again we've been eating take-out from the restaurants in town." The housekeeper leaned across the island and whispered, "Don't tell your mama, but I'm glad she's taking a break from the kitchen."

"I thought you loved my mother's cooking."

"I do. But lately she's been on a health kick. Worried about our hearts and cholesterol." Eunice grimaced. "We eat so many vegetables now my skin's turning green."

Maria and Riley laughed.

"I snuck into town last week and had me a Big Mac." Eunice smacked her lips. "Thought I'd died and gone to heaven."

"What time is dinner tonight?" Riley asked.

"Seven. Don't be late." Eunice turned to Maria. "Have Riley put your things in the yellow bedroom at the top of the stairs. We keep that room clean in case we have an unexpected guest." Eunice glanced at the wall clock above the sink. "Time for my nap. Holler if you two need anything."

"Thank you, Eunice."

The housekeeper patted Maria's hand. "No trouble at all, Miss Maria."

"She's a lovely woman," Maria said as soon as Eunice left the kitchen.

"I have a lot of happy memories at Belle Farms."

"I'm surprised you'd want to leave this place."

"I don't have the same passion for horse racing that my father and sister have." Riley stood. "Speaking of fathers and sisters…ready to meet mine?"

"Sure." Maria followed Riley out the back door, then along a stone path. She took in the bustling activity around her—trainers walking horses in and out of barns. Hay bales being unloaded from a truck. A horse being hosed down. Another groomed and yet another examined by a veterinarian.

Riley left the path and approached an enclosed pen where a young woman guided a horse through a series of jumps in an obstacle course.

"I thought your family was into racing," Maria said.

"My sister competes in show jumping in her spare time. She's training Princess Leia." Bree sat tall and straight in the saddle, a long red braid swishing across her back. She coaxed the beautiful brown-and-white mare over three gates, then turned a corner and leapt across a water hazard, before slowing the animal to a trot.

"Riley!" Bree reined in Princess Leia in front of the fence, then hopped off and swatted the mare's rump. The horse trotted away.

Bree slipped through the rails and brother and sister bear-hugged. Maria felt a twinge of envy, their closeness reminding her of how much she missed her brother. Pasting a polite smile on her face she waited for an introduction.

"I want you to meet a very special friend of mine— Maria Alvarez."

"Hello." Bree scowled at Riley. "Mom never mentioned that you were bringing a guest tonight."

Maria's stomach plummeted. Why hadn't Riley sought his parents' permission before inviting her on the trip?

"I wanted to surprise Mom and Dad." Riley slid his arm around Maria's waist and pulled her next to him. "Maria and I met in Albuquerque when my plane went down."

"Went down?" Bree's eyes widened. "Dad never mentioned you'd had trouble with the plane."

"He doesn't know, so keep my secret, okay?"

"What happened?"

"Bird strike. I landed the plane in an abandoned salvage yard."

Bree's expression grew more horrified by the second and Maria wished Riley would spare his sister the particulars.

"Maria happened to be checking on her students

who were waiting in the salvage yard for a gang called the—"

"I'm sure Bree doesn't care to hear all the boring details," Maria interrupted. "My father's an airplane mechanic and he worked on Riley's plane."

"Oh." A curious expression remained on Bree's face, but she refrained from prying. No doubt she'd corner her brother later and badger him with questions.

"Good thing you didn't cancel at the last minute. Dad's worried the deal with Mr. Westin will fall through. He expects you to charm the pants off him and Serena."

"Serena?" Riley asked.

Maria was all ears.

"Mom didn't tell you?" Bree glanced between her brother and Maria. "Serena's Mr. Westin's daughter. She's a concert pianist."

"Why was she invited to the dinner?" Riley asked.

"Why do you think?" Bree batted her eyelashes. "Mom's matchmaking again." She flashed Maria an apologetic smile. "If Mom had known Riley was bringing you, she wouldn't have invited Serena."

"No worries. Riley and I are just friends." Maybe if she said it aloud enough times, Maria's heart would believe it.

"Good. Then there won't be any awkwardness." Bree hugged her brother a second time. "It was nice to meet you, Maria. I'll see you at dinner."

As soon as Bree was out of earshot, Maria hissed, "How could you, Riley?"

"How could I what?"

"First, you didn't tell your parents I was coming and now they've invited a woman to the dinner who expects you—"

"Expects me to what?" Riley inched closer to Maria.

Flustered, Maria glared. "To be unattached." She couldn't be with Riley, but, darn it, she didn't want any other woman to be with him, either.

You can't have your cake and eat it, too.

"I had no idea that my mother invited Mr. Westin's daughter. When I spoke to my father several weeks ago he never mentioned Serena."

"I'll keep Eunice company in the kitchen while you entertain the *pianist*." Maria swallowed a groan at the waspish tone in her voice.

"Jealous?"

"Absolutely not."

"My mother's been playing matchmaker since she introduced Amy to me," Riley said.

Good grief. Why did Riley have to bring up his old flame?

"Mom and Amy's dad were friends in college. You know—" Riley waved his hand in the air "—the whole sorority-fraternity thing."

No, Maria did not know the whole sorority-fraternity thing.

"They remained good friends through the years even after they'd married other people. Mom was pretty angry at me for ruining things with Amy."

Maria sympathized with Riley's mother. She must have been embarrassed by her son's infidelity.

"Mom believes she knows what's best for me—but when it comes to women, only I know the kind of woman I want." Riley's confession sent Maria's heart tumbling. "Will you let me tell you what happened between me and Amy?"

If she didn't, he'd never drop the subject. In truth,

Maria was curious about Riley's affair with Amy. "Give me the shortened version."

"I cheated on Amy."

"I know. Amy told me." Maria expected Riley to fire off one excuse after another for his actions. He surprised her.

"My feelings for Amy began to weaken the second semester of my senior year of college. I was focused on rodeo and making plans to ride the circuit after graduation. I spent less and less time with her and—" he shrugged "—I expected her to realize our relationship had run its course."

"Why didn't you tell Amy you wanted to break up?" Maria had questioned why Fernando hadn't told her he'd fallen out of love with her. It would have hurt Maria but at least she'd have been spared the humiliation of having been cheated on.

"I realize I should have made it clear to Amy that I didn't want to be with her anymore, but I took the easy path, hoping she'd figure it out on her own."

"But she didn't until you cheated on her."

"I'm not proud of hurting Amy with a one-night stand."

Maria didn't know if a one-night stand was better or worse than an affair.

Riley stared down at the grass. "I know what I did was wrong. I'm not going to make excuses for myself or say that I was immature. But I've learned from my mistakes and I'd never intentionally hurt you, Maria."

Intentionally being the key word.

"Maria." He clasped her hand. "I invited you to Belle Farms because I want my parents to meet the woman who makes me happy. The woman I want to be with. The woman I intend to be faithful to."

Heart crawling up into her throat, Maria struggled to speak. Before a word came out of her mouth, Riley said, "There's my dad."

Chapter Thirteen

"Did you break the news to Mom, yet?" Riley had asked his father to warn his mother about Maria before their dinner guests arrived.

"I did." The lines bracketing his father's mouth deepened.

The two men stood outside on the patio waiting for Westin and his daughter. Lantern lights swung from the trees and four umbrella heaters placed strategically around the space warded off the chill in the evening air. "What did Mom say?"

"She's not happy, so do me a favor and be nice to Westin's daughter."

"And ignore Maria?" *Not a chance.*

"Maria's older than you, isn't she?"

"Ten years."

His father's scowl deepened.

"The age difference doesn't bother me, Dad. Maria's an intriguing woman."

"She mentioned being a teacher."

"Maria tutors at-risk teens."

"Challenging work."

And not safe.

"Why isn't she in a traditional school classroom?" his father asked.

Without going into detail, Riley said, "She wants inner-city kids to have a better life. She's a crusader."

"Crusaders don't make much money."

Increasing the family coffers was his father's passion in life—the reason he and Riley didn't see eye-to-eye.

"Have you decided what you'll do after the finals in Vegas?"

"Yes." Riley had done a lot of soul-searching while flying from rodeo to rodeo the past few weeks. The one thing he knew for certain was that he wouldn't be returning to Belle Farms. "Horse racing has been part of our family for generations and I want Belle Farms to flourish, but I'm not the right man to carry on for you."

"Belle Farms provided you with a privileged life."

"And I appreciate all it's given me, but instead of making more money I'd rather spend what I have helping others."

"You're talking philanthropy work?"

"Something along those lines."

"I'm listening."

Riley had a plan in mind even though he hadn't worked out all the details. "I'm thinking of purchasing a working ranch where at-risk teens can get a second chance to turn their lives around while earning their high-school diplomas." He braced himself for his father's objection. One never came. "If Belle Farms helped sponsor the ranch, the publicity would go a long way with the racing public," Riley added.

"I'm guessing this ranch would be near Albuquerque."

"Yes." Maria was an integral part of Riley's plan and he refused to consider that she might not want to be involved with his project.

"I'll consider your idea. In the meantime where are you spending Thanksgiving?"

Riley was holding out for an invitation to join Maria and her family. "I'm not sure yet."

"Your mother and I have decided to visit her cousin in San Diego for the holiday. Bree's staying here to watch over the farm. Keep Eunice posted about your plans. She'll be around to cook if you want to spend the holiday at home."

Home. Since Riley had met Maria, Belle Farms didn't feel like home anymore. "I'll know what I'm doing shortly."

"If you're—"

Riley turned to see what had interrupted his father. Through the windows along the back of the house Riley spotted Maria chatting with his mother in the kitchen. Maria wore a knee-length red cocktail dress with spaghetti straps. The satiny bodice hugged her breasts and the pleated skirt swirled around her hips. Red high heels added a few inches to her height and to-night she'd styled her hair in curls that bounced against her bare shoulders.

"Well," his father murmured. "I can see why you find her attractive."

"She thinks I'm too young for her."

"Smart woman."

"Dad, I'm a competitor. It's only a matter of time before I persuade her that we belong together."

"You're that serious about her?"

"I'm surer of Maria than I am of winning the title in

December." Riley set his beer down and went to meet her as she stepped onto the patio.

The first words out of her mouth were "I met your mother."

The first words out of his mouth were "You're beautiful."

"Did you hear what I said?"

He threaded his fingers through hers. "What happened?"

"Your mother was very polite to me but I can tell she isn't pleased about my presence tonight. Riley, I think it would be best if I waited in my bedroom until dinner is over and the guests leave."

"No. You're staying by my side." Right then the back door opened and Riley's mother escorted Pete Westin and his daughter outside. Riley eyed Serena from head-to-toe and in less than three seconds decided his mother had missed the mark again. The blonde wasn't his type.

"Pete, good to see you again," Riley's father said to the former rodeo cowboy. "This is my son, Riley, and his friend Maria Alvarez."

"Heard you're chasing a second title this year," Westin said.

"Not many cowboys can match your success, Mr. Westin."

The former rodeo star preened at the compliment. "This here's my daughter, Serena. She graduated from Yale and recently returned from touring overseas."

"My mother said you're a gifted pianist," Riley said.

"I'm afraid I was destined for a career in music." Serena smiled. "My mother tied me to the piano bench because she was afraid I'd follow in my father's footsteps and become a cowgirl."

"You ladies won't mind if we men discuss business before dinner?" Riley's father said.

"Of course not." Riley's mother slipped her arm through Serena's. "I want to hear all about your concerts in Europe."

Riley waggled his eyebrows at Maria then followed his father and Mr. Westin.

"Oh, dear," Riley's mother said. "That was the doorbell. If you'll excuse me a minute, I believe the caterers have arrived."

Left alone with Serena, Maria asked, "Would you care for a drink?"

They walked over to the built-in grill and bar. Maria picked out a bottle of red wine and Serena said, "That's fine." She glanced around. "Belle Farms is very impressive. Do you visit often?"

"This is my first time here." Maria handed Serena a wineglass.

"Do you know much about horse racing?"

"Not a thing."

"I don't particularly care one way or another about the sport." Serena nodded to the men. "Your cowboy is very hot."

"Riley's a great guy, but he's not my cowboy."

"I do love their swaggers, but I wish my father would stop trying to marry me off to a cowboy." Serena sipped her wine. "I prefer city life over country living."

After all her visits to the Gateway Ranch, Maria had grown fond of fresh air and wide-open spaces.

"Riley hasn't stopped staring at you since we walked over here," Serena whispered.

Maria resisted the urge to glance over her shoulder. "We're friends."

"Friends with sleeping privileges?"

"We're too different to make a long-term relationship work." Maria was saved from having to explain when Riley's sister arrived outside. Following introductions Bree launched into a conversation about the farm's past Kentucky Derby winners.

Dinner was less stressful than Maria anticipated mainly because talk centered on rodeo and horse racing. Riley's mother attempted to change the subject to Serena's concert tours but Serena didn't cooperate, which amused Maria. The men declined dessert and disappeared into the library to conclude their business deal while the women remained at the table and devoured slices of cheesecake drizzled with raspberry sauce. Following dessert Bree excused herself to check on the horses and Serena offered to play the piano.

A half hour later the men emerged from the library flashing smug grins. Shortly afterward, Serena and her father departed and Riley's mother pleaded a headache then retreated to her bedroom. Time for Maria to retire to her room. She held out her hand to Riley's father. "It was very nice to meet you, Mr. Fitzgerald. Belle Farms is a beautiful piece of paradise and I enjoyed seeing Riley's childhood home."

"You're not turning in already, are you?" Riley asked.

"You and your father should have time to talk." Maria retreated to the guest bedroom, relieved to avoid further scrutiny. She had her dress unzipped halfway when the door flew open.

"Riley!"

He closed the door then leaned against it. "What's the matter?"

"Nothing. I thought you'd want time alone with your father since we're leaving early in the morning."

"I want time alone with you." He crossed the carpet and stood before her.

"Kissing isn't a good idea," Maria warned as his mouth drew near.

Riley stared at her. Seconds passed, their mouths inches apart, then he abruptly pulled back. "Let's get this over with."

"Get what over with?"

"You refusing to accept that you're in love with me," he said.

Where did Riley get off…

Dear God. It was true, wasn't it? She was in love with Riley.

"I'll go first." The blue of his eyes deepened. "I'm in love with you, Maria."

Rattled, she struggled to collect her thoughts, an impossible task after Riley's confession. "We can't."

"Can't what? Love each other?"

Why did he insist on making this so difficult? "We're too different. A long-term relationship would never last."

"Different how?"

Was he kidding? "I'm ten years older than you, Riley."

"Ten years isn't much these days. Besides, older women-younger men marriages are more common than they used to be."

Marriages? "I'm not ready for this." Maria pressed her hand to her thumping heart, angry she'd opened the door to questions about her past—humiliating questions she didn't care to answer.

"What did he do to you, Maria?"

Tell him. Then he'll finally understand.

"Fernando said he didn't want children—"

"Who's Fernando?"

Maria moved across the room, putting the bed between her and Riley. "My ex-fiancé."

"I'm listening."

"Since Fernando and I worked all day with at-risk teens we decided we wouldn't have enough emotional energy left at the end of the day to raise our own children."

"And…"

"Fernando changed his mind and wanted kids. We argued a lot about it."

"But you refused to reconsider having a family."

Damn you, Riley, you're going to make me say it, aren't you? "Yes. What happened to my brother left me with a deep scar. I don't want children because I won't risk losing them."

Riley's expression gentled as if he'd known her fears all along.

"Fernando dropped the subject of having kids and I assumed we'd settled the matter. Then he met a woman. They had an affair and she got pregnant."

"Do you think he got her pregnant on purpose so he could have a child?"

That's exactly what she'd accused Fernando of doing, although he'd denied the charge. "I don't know."

"I'm sorry he hurt you, Maria." Riley skirted the end of the bed and put his arms around her. "I can understand why you'd be afraid to have children but don't you believe you'll feel differently once you hold your own baby in your arms?"

"Of course I would feel differently. That's why I can't allow myself to fall in love." She brushed a lock of hair from Riley's forehead, knowing that if she gave her heart to him he'd have the power to make her change her mind about having a baby—his baby. "You need a haircut."

"Don't change the subject," he said.

"At twenty-five, most men your age aren't thinking about marriage, let alone fatherhood." She pressed a finger to his mouth when he attempted to protest. "One day, maybe in your thirties, you'll be ready to start a family. And I would be in my forties."

"Lots of women get pregnant in their forties. Look at all the movie stars who—"

"It's not simply age, Riley. There are cultural differences we've ignored until now."

"You're prejudiced?"

"I'm referring to our parents. Neither of them would have picked us for each other. And if family approval means nothing to you then the fact that our lives are going in different directions should be a cause for concern."

"I'm not going to rodeo forever."

"I realize that, but I *am* going to help inner-city teens forever. I've found my calling and it's right in my own backyard. I'll never leave Albuquerque."

Riley released Maria and walked to the door. He paused with his hand on the knob. "Your arguments are sound, but you forgot one thing."

"What's that?"

"You didn't take into account that you've already fallen in love with me and you don't want to live without me." The quiet click of the door followed his statement.

Maria battled tears. Riley had guessed the truth—she did love him. What she'd felt for Fernando paled in comparison to her feelings for Riley. She worshipped the ground the cowboy walked on for all he'd done to help Cruz, Victor and Alonso. If she took a chance on Riley and their relationship didn't last or if tragedy struck and she lost him… Maria wasn't strong enough to survive losing another man she'd come to love.

"THANKS FOR COMING HOME WITH me," Riley said, breaking the strained silence that accompanied their flight back to Albuquerque.

"I enjoyed meeting your family." Their goodbyes to Riley's parents had been stilted but polite. Both had invited her to return for another visit when she and Riley had more time, but Maria sensed their reservations about their son's involvement with her.

Riley guided the *Dark Stranger* into a hangar at Blue Skies Regional Airport then cut the engine. He grabbed Maria's hand when she attempted to unhook the seat harness. "We need to talk."

Fearing she'd break down and cry if Riley pleaded his case again, she shook her head.

"You're not even willing to give us a chance?"

It wouldn't work, Riley.

"I need you, Maria. You're a strong, generous champion for the kids that society has cast aside." He shoved a hand through his hair. "Don't you see? You inspire me to be a better man."

Her eyes watered.

"People view me as a rich, spoiled guy who doesn't have to work for anything. No one gives me credit for my rodeo talent. They insist that it's easy for me to succeed because wealth gives me advantages most cowboys can't match. I fly to rodeos instead of driving long hours. I sleep in the best hotels instead of my truck. I don't have to hire on at ranches between rodeos to earn entry-fee money. Instead, I can rest and allow my injuries to heal."

Heart aching, Maria hated seeing Riley upset.

"You're the first person who sees beyond my wealth to who I am in here." He thumped his fist against his chest. "I don't want to lose you, Maria. Give me a chance to make you happy."

Maria was too torn inside to speak.

"I know Albuquerque is your home. I'm willing to make it my home, too."

She had to escape from the plane before she gave in to Riley's impassioned plea. "I'm sorry." Her voice cracked. She scrambled from her seat, leaving Riley no choice but to unlock the door and lower the steps. As soon as he joined her on the tarmac he pulled her into his arms.

Her defenses decimated, Maria melted against him.

"I love you," he whispered. "I honest-to-God, seriously, with-all-my-heart love you."

Maria loved Riley more than she'd ever loved Fernando and she'd be devastated if one day Riley woke and decided she was too old for him. Or that she didn't excite him anymore. Or that he was tired of her devoting all her time and energy to at-risk kids and not him. And if her parents eventually accepted Riley, Maria feared they'd view him as a replacement for the son they'd lost. Then one day when Riley decided he'd had enough of being tied down to Maria and left, her parents would lose a second son.

Riley's mouth crushed Maria's, awakening her desire. She tasted desperation on his tongue and her heart wept at the hurt she was inflicting on him. A throat clearing startled them and Riley ended the kiss. Maria's father stood ten feet away, glaring.

"Mr. Alvarez."

"I was saying goodbye to Riley, Dad. He's heading out to the ranch, so I'll have to hitch a ride home with you."

Maria spun but Riley grabbed her elbow. "Remember, Cruz is competing in the El Paso junior rodeo at the end of the month. Victor and Alonso are welcome to tag along if it's okay with their parents."

"I'll check in to it."

"Nice seeing you again, sir," Riley said. He shifted toward Maria and she swore his blue eyes glistened with moisture. "'Bye, Maria."

Once Riley left the hangar, her father spoke. "Have you no shame?"

"I'm not in the mood, Dad."

"If your mother knew you were involved with a man your brother's age—"

"Riley's a great guy. Yes, he's the same age as Juan would have been had he lived, but why should that matter? Riley is decent, caring and he's genuinely concerned about the boys I'm trying to help."

"Those boys are a waste of time. They'll end up dead. The same as your brother."

"I never thought you'd remain bitter the rest of your life."

"You don't know the pain of losing your only son."

"Is that why you and Mom don't want me to be happy? You want me to be as miserable as you two the rest of my life?" She waited for her father to deny the accusation. He didn't. They headed for his truck in the parking lot, Maria's feet dragging—guilt, anger and sadness weighing them down.

Chapter Fourteen

"Thanks for all the bucking lessons." Cruz spoke to Riley inside the barn where the two males organized and stowed the teen's rodeo equipment. "I didn't think you were gonna be here this week. Ms. Alvarez said you were too busy competing to help me get ready for El Paso."

"I had to withdraw from a rodeo." Riley had hated walking away from another win but he'd hated even more the idea of giving up on him and Maria. Thoughts of Maria had begun to interfere with his concentration and he'd decided to return to Albuquerque and remind Maria why they were meant to be together. The only problem with his plan was that Maria was nowhere to be found. She wasn't returning his calls and she hadn't stopped at the ranch since he'd arrived six days ago. She couldn't avoid him forever—the junior rodeo was tomorrow.

"Why'd you withdraw?" Cruz asked.

"Sore shoulder." He rubbed his arm.

Cruz narrowed his eyes. "You said the best of the best ride with injuries."

"They do." Riley shrugged. "I can afford to sit out a rodeo with a small purse."

"How much was first place worth?"

"A grand."

"That's a lot of money." The comment came from the other end of the barn, where Victor held a pitchfork in his hand. Shorty must have assigned the teen to muck stalls.

"Mind if I have a word alone with Victor?" Riley spoke to Cruz.

"Yeah, sure." Cruz left the barn.

"You and I need to talk, Victor."

The kid tossed a pitchfork-full of soiled hay into the wheelbarrow, narrowly missing Riley. "Talk about what?"

"Ms. Alvarez believes I'm a bad influence on you." Riley wondered if Maria was using her concern over Riley spending time with the teens as an excuse to keep him from getting too close to her.

"What do you mean a bad influence?" Victor asked.

"Heard you were trying to get into the Los Locos gang."

"So."

"You think that's a smart idea?"

"I earned my GED. You and Ms. Alvarez can't tell me what to do anymore." Another clump of dirty hay flew past Riley's head.

"You're better than a thug, Victor."

"The Los Locos aren't thugs. Besides, I can make a lot of cash being a lookout for the gang and—" Victor spread his arms wide "—I can be somebody important. I don't have to be a nobody my whole life."

"There are other ways to make a name for yourself aside from joining a gang and breaking laws."

"Who says I'm gonna break the law?" Victor's chin

lifted defiantly. "Don't matter none 'cause nobody cares what I do anyway."

"Ms. Alvarez and I care."

A rude bark of laughter erupted from the kid's mouth. "The only reason you're even here is because of Ms. Alvarez. You're helping us 'cause *you* like her."

"What's wrong with that?"

Silence.

"Ever thought about using your GED to enroll in a community college or study to be a plumber? You can make good money in the trades."

"Why should I work my butt off for a few bucks when I can rake in the dough being a lookout for the Los Locos?" Victor straightened his shoulders and grinned. "I wanna wallet full of hundred-dollar bills like yours."

Score a point for Maria. Victor had noticed the way Riley spread money around. He didn't have the right to tell the kid he had to work hard for his money when Riley hadn't earned a dime of the funds he had access to.

"What if you had the opportunity to make a lot of money doing honest work?"

"How much money?"

"What will the Los Locos pay you?"

"I don't know. A Benjamin or two."

"A hundred dollars an hour? A day? A week? Or a month?"

"I don't know."

Riley doubted Victor would earn any substantial amount of money in the gang. He'd be lucky if the group repaid his service by buying him a fast-food meal. "What will you do with that much money?"

"Shoot, man, I'm gonna buy me a jacked-up car

with a kick-ass stereo." Victor wiggled his fingers.
"Maybe get me some bling."

Fancy gold necklaces and rings would only make
Victor a target for rival gang members. "Will you miss
working at the ranch after you leave?"

"Nah." Victor shrugged. "Maybe a little."

"What will you miss the most?"

"Not shoveling horseshit, that's for sure."

"I'm serious."

"I'd miss Shorty."

"I thought Shorty made you work too hard."

"He does. But he gives a crap about me—I mean
people. He's not prejudiced against Latinos and he says
I do a good job."

"You think the Los Locos will treat you with the
same respect?" Riley asked. "What if you screw up?
Will the gang give you a second or third chance like
Shorty does?"

Victor didn't have an answer to that question.

"Life isn't easy—"

"What would you know about easy? You fly a plane
and have a ton of money. I bet you've never had to go
a whole day without eating 'cause you had no money
and your mom hadn't been to the grocery store in over
a month."

"You're right. I've never gone hungry. But think
about this, Victor. We have no control over what family
we're born into. No control over our ethnicity or how
our parents earn a living or where they live."

"You got lucky, man."

"I agree. I'm fortunate and blessed. My ancestors
struggled and went hungry so that I didn't have to.
They didn't break the law—they broke a sweat and

shed their own tears and blood to leave a legacy for future generations. You can do the same."

"What are you talking about?"

"Put your GED to good use. Carve out your own path in life. Show your siblings that working hard at an honest job is the way to get what you want. Be a role model for your friends and family."

"Me, a role model? Get real, man."

"Think about it, Victor. You've got the brains to succeed at whatever you choose to do. Leave your mark on the world not on the side of a building. Dream about being more than you ever believed you could be."

"Dreams don't matter none if you don't have a way to make 'em come true."

"Nothing worth having comes easy." Riley shuffled his feet. "Think about what I've said. Once you join the Los Locos there's no turning back. The life you could have had will be lost to you forever."

"My life ain't gonna last long anyway, so why should I care about how I make my money? I'm never gonna get out of the 'hood. Might as well take the easy money and party before a bullet takes me down." Victor tossed the pitchfork into the stall and pushed the wheelbarrow out a side door that led to the compost bin behind the barn. If Victor didn't place any value on his own life, the teen would never believe he deserved better than a day-to-day existence in the 'hood.

Riley believed each time Maria lost a student to a gang she was forced to relive her brother's death. The thought of her experiencing that kind of pain over and over again twisted Riley's gut. Right then Riley decided that if he couldn't be a ray of hope in Maria's life, he wouldn't be in her life at all.

MARIA SMILED AT THE EXCITEMENT on the teens' faces as they entered Fifer's Arena in El Paso, Texas. True to his word, Riley had returned to Albuquerque at the end of October for Cruz's first junior rodeo competition.

She wasn't happy that Riley ignored her request to keep his distance from the boys, but at the same time she admired him for keeping his promise to Cruz and helping him prepare for the rodeo. Because she'd missed Riley more than she'd ever believed possible, Maria hadn't trust herself to be around him so she'd avoided the Gateway Ranch.

When Riley arrived at the Blue Skies Regional Airport earlier in the morning, she'd waited for him to turn his smile on her, but he ignored her and greeted everyone else. If he'd been surprised that her father and Judge Hamel were tagging along, he hadn't said a word.

Maria had persuaded her father to attend the rodeo, hoping he'd witness a different side of the teens and acknowledge the importance of her work.

"Good luck, Cruz," Maria said. "We'll be cheering for you in the stands."

Cruz caught Maria by surprise and hugged her. "Thanks for not giving up on me, Ms. Alvarez."

He turned to Judge Hamel and offered his hand. Cruz's court hearing had been two weeks earlier and had lasted all of five minutes. Judge Hamel had given Cruz a stern warning to stay away from gangs and that if he appeared in her courtroom again she'd send him to jail. "Thank you for giving me a second chance."

"You're welcome, young man." The judge pumped his hand. "Make us proud."

Cruz bumped knuckles with Victor and Alonso. "This one's for all the homies in the 'hood."

Riley motioned for Cruz to follow him to the bucking chutes and Maria led the way to their seats.

"Maria, I'm impressed with the changes in Cruz. What you're doing with these kids is terrific," Judge Hamel said.

"Thank you." Although Maria's father pretended interest in the rodeo clowns entertaining the fans, she sensed that he had eavesdropped on her conversation with the judge.

"I'm amazed by parents of teens who pass through my chambers, insisting they had no idea their kid had been involved in a gang. Parents are notorious for blaming others rather than acknowledging they should have paid closer attention to their child's activities."

"The allure of gangs is difficult to resist when gangbangers make big bucks, drive fancy cars and wear diamond rings and expensive clothes," Maria said. "And they get a kick out of people fearing them."

"Well, at least you're making progress with a few of the kids." Judge Hamel stood. "I'm going to the restroom before the action starts."

Once the judge was out of earshot, Maria turned to her father. "What's the matter, Dad? You're awfully quiet. Aren't you feeling well?"

"I'm sorry, *cariño.*"

Surprised by his statement, Maria asked, "Sorry for what?"

"For blaming you when your mother and I should have realized Juan had fallen in with the wrong crowd."

"Dad, Judge Hamel made a generalization—"

"Don't make excuses for me, daughter. I was Juan's father. I should have known his friends." The folds around his mouth sagged with sadness. "Your brother stared me in the eye and lied about where he was going. I knew he lied but I didn't want to believe it."

"If we could turn back the clock, we'd all make different decisions. I tried to help Juan but in all the wrong ways."

Her father clutched her hand. "You were a good sister."

Stunned by her father's turnaround, Maria said, "It's too late for Juan, but there's time for them." She pointed to Victor and Alonso, sitting two rows away. "I see Juan in the eyes of every boy I help. There are so many good kids who make bad choices."

"The hurt never goes away." Her father sniffed.

"I know."

"Your mother will never stop drinking."

Maria ached for her parents' marriage. Her father had not only lost a son but he'd also lost the woman he'd married over thirty years ago. "You could help me make a difference, Dad. You could be a mentor for at-risk teens."

His eyes narrowed. "How?"

"You could teach boys and girls about airplane mechanics and discuss your career in the military."

"*Sí.* I will think about it."

She hugged her father. For ten long years, he'd buried his anger and guilt over his son's death. Today marked a new beginning for their relationship.

And you have Riley to thank for this moment.

Maybe it was time Maria admitted that Riley's presence did more good than harm to those he touched. Yes, Victor intended to take a shortcut to living the high life, but Maria doubted the boys would have earned their GEDs if they'd remained in the 'hood. Riley had provided the teens with a safe environment to study and work away from the influence of gangs. Shorty and the Gateway Ranch had brought about positive changes in all three boys.

Judge Hamel returned to her seat and a moment later the announcer's voice bellowed over the loudspeakers. "Ladies and gents, it's time to begin our pro-am junior rodeo!"

Hoping to catch a glimpse of Riley and Cruz, Maria scanned the chute area.

"We've got twelve young men here today who're waiting to strut their stuff on a few ill-mannered bucking horses."

"Got any questions?" Riley asked Cruz as they stood next to Dark Magic's chute.

The corner of Cruz's mouth curved. "Yeah, how do I keep from falling off again?"

Even though Cruz joked, he couldn't conceal the fear in his eyes. Riley had experienced the same jitters the first time he'd competed. "Stick like glue to the saddle and you won't take a tumble."

"If I don't do well, I can't blame it on my equipment," Cruz said.

Riley had heard kids gossiping with envy over Cruz's saddle. They'd probably had to scrape and save for a year to buy second-hand gear in order to compete today and in walks the new kid with expensive equipment and a world-champion sponsor.

"Shut them up," Riley said.

"If Judge Hamel catches me fighting, she's gonna throw me in jail."

"I'm not suggesting a brawl." Riley chuckled. "Ride well and win." Winning was the only way to silence the critics.

Cruz scaled the chute rails and straddled the bronc. "I think I'm ready."

"You're more than ready. Remember, when Dark Magic makes his move out of the chute, keep your spurs above his shoulders until he completes his first jump. Don't forget to lift the buck rein and keep spurring the horse front-to-back finishing behind the saddle."

"Got it," Cruz said.

"One more thing," Riley said.

"What?"

"Have fun."

Cruz fiddled with the black Stetson Shorty had given him for good luck then signaled the gateman. Dark Magic bolted from the chute and Riley watched the kid mark out.

Six seconds...

Dark Magic wasn't anywhere near the size and strength of the broncs Riley rode but the young horse was riled. The animal spun twice then bucked his back legs high off the ground, forcing Cruz to use every ounce of his strength to remain in the saddle.

Three seconds...

Another series of spins and bucks.

Two seconds...

The bronc rocked forward and Riley guessed what was to come.

One second...

Dark Magic used the momentum he'd built for his final buck, which brought all four hooves off the ground. The front of the bronc rolled right, testing Cruz's physical agility. The kid slid but managed to cling to his seat.

The buzzer sounded and Cruz jumped off Dark

Magic, landing on his feet. The crowd cheered his performance and Riley never felt prouder as he watched the teen's face glow with pride.

"That was such a rush!" Cruz pumped his fist in the air.

"You've got what it takes to be one of the best, kid. You have to decide how bad you want it."

"I know."

"Here come a few people who want to congratulate you." Riley couldn't take his eyes off Maria. Today she wore her hair down, the dark strands brushing her shoulders. Her jeans and long-sleeved blouse weren't fancy but they hugged her shape, showing off her curves. She was a beautiful woman. A woman he wanted for himself.

Her eyes shimmered with emotion and he hoped she'd missed him as much as he'd missed her. While the others congratulated Cruz, Riley inched closer to Maria. He yearned to take her in his arms. Hold her. Kiss her. Instead, he clenched his hands into fists to keep from grabbing her.

"Thanks to you, Cruz might have a career in rodeo," she said.

Riley didn't want to discuss Cruz or rodeo. He wanted to talk about them—their future. "I've decided this is going to be my final run at another title. Whether I win or not in December I'm leaving the circuit."

"Why?"

"I've got other interests—" *people* "—I want to pursue." And he'd devised a plan on how to convince Maria that *he* was integral to her mission to prove to at-risk teens that education not gangs was the path to a better life. But until he worked out the details and gained his father's approval, he didn't want to raise Maria's hopes. "I'll be on the road until the finals in Vegas the first week of December." He wished she'd give him a sign that she'd miss him, but her schooled expression hid her thoughts.

"I'll be cheering for you in Vegas," Maria said.

If all went as planned, Maria would be cheering for him in person in Vegas.

Chapter Fifteen

"Thanks for the lift, Ms. Alvarez." Victor hopped into Maria's station wagon and buckled his seat belt.

"You're welcome. I'm glad you decided to come along." A week ago Gil Parker had invited her and Victor to Thanksgiving dinner at the Gateway Ranch. "Cruz and Alonso will be glad to see you."

"Yeah, I guess."

After the junior rodeo in El Paso, Cruz and Alonso had asked Gil Parker if they could continue to work at the ranch. Cruz wanted to hone his rodeo skills and Alonso wanted to prepare for the SAT and ACT college entrance exams he intended to take in the spring. Gil had extended an invite to remain at the ranch to Victor, but the teen declined, citing that he couldn't wait to return to the 'hood.

"How are things going?" she asked.

"You mean with the Los Locos?"

Maria clenched the wheel tighter. "Yes."

"I didn't join the gang," Victor said matter-of-factly.

Startled, Maria glanced at the teen. "How come?"

"I thought a lot about what Riley said."

Riley hadn't phoned her since El Paso...since *forever.* "When did you speak with him?"

"Before Cruz's rodeo."

"What did Riley tell you?"

"He said I should dream big—bigger than the Los Locos. And I told him that it didn't matter what my dreams were 'cause I didn't have a way to make 'em come true."

"Nothing worth having comes easy," Maria said.

"That's what Riley said, Ms. Alvarez. He told me that once I joined a gang I couldn't change my mind and my life wouldn't belong to me anymore. It would belong to the Los Locos."

Bless you, Riley. He'd been able to reach Victor when she'd failed.

"He told me I was better than a thug."

"He's right."

"And Riley said we can't help what family we're born into or who our parents are. It's up to me to show my brothers and sisters that we can change how we live if we want to bad enough."

"So what are your plans?" Maria asked.

"I'm gonna ask Mr. Parker if he'll let me come back to the ranch. I wanna work with the horses and maybe if I do a good job for Shorty, Mr. Parker will let me be a real ranch hand for him one day."

Oh, Riley, why did I ever doubt you? Maria blinked back tears. "I'm proud of you, Victor."

"Thanks, Ms. Alvarez. Is Riley gonna be at the ranch for Thanksgiving dinner?"

"I don't know." She hadn't asked Gil because she'd been afraid to learn the truth—that Riley had washed his hands of her.

A half hour later, Maria and Victor learned that Riley would not be present. He was in Florida riding in one last rodeo before the finals the first week in December. Maria hid her disappointment behind a brave smile.

Supper in the bunkhouse was a lively affair. Harriet sat on Gil's right. The couple bent their head in conversation throughout the meal and Maria sensed there was more to their relationship than boss and employee and the knowledge made Maria miss Riley even more.

Not a day went by since El Paso that Maria hadn't been tempted to contact Riley. She'd stayed busy working with a new group of students, but at the end of the day she returned to her parents' home feeling empty inside. Before she'd met Riley she'd been content to devote her life to troubled teens, but now she believed there was more to life than helping others. She was entitled to her own happiness.

Maria had finally accepted that the key to her happiness was Riley. All of a sudden their ten-year age difference no longer mattered. Life was short—very short in the 'hood. She wanted to live each day to the fullest and she couldn't do that without Riley by her side.

"Hey, Ms. Alvarez, what do you think of Victor's new snake tattoo?" Alonso said.

Maria stared at Victor's forearm. "It's ugly."

The cowboys around the table chuckled and Shorty teased Victor about his baggy jeans. Victor took it all in stride and Maria was pleased to see that the boys had truly become part of the ranch family. Following supper, Pete served coffee and dessert—a variety of cobblers, pies and cookies.

"I'll be right back," Gil announced. He returned to the bunkhouse a few minutes later carrying a large box wrapped in shiny red Christmas paper with a fancy white ribbon. He set the box in front of Maria. "This came for you a few days ago."

Maria's eyes widened. "From who?"

"Riley."

Maria's heart thumped wildly in her chest.

"Riley got you a Christmas present, Ms. Alvarez!" Alonso said.

"Hurry and open it. Maybe it's a new bucking saddle," Cruz said.

"I doubt he bought me rodeo gear." Maria laughed.

"Want me to help?" Victor asked.

"Sure." Maria clutched her hands in her lap and watched as the boys tore off the ribbon and paper.

Cruz lifted the lid. "There's another box inside."

Alonso removed a medium-size box wrapped with the same paper and identical white ribbon.

"You'll have to open that one." Maria's heart beat faster.

"Uh-oh. Another box," Alonso said.

The ranch hands placed bets on how many more boxes the boys would uncover.

When Victor opened the next one, which was the size of a candy box, he discovered six plane tickets to Las Vegas dated December ninth—the day before Riley's final ride. Each of the boys' names was on a ticket as was Maria's and her parents'.

"Does this mean we all get to go to Vegas to watch Riley at the NFR?" Cruz asked.

"I believe it does." If Maria's heart pounded any harder, the organ would explode inside her chest.

"There's one more box hiding in here." Cruz handed Maria a small red-wrapped box with a tiny white ribbon around it.

Maria unraveled the ribbon and carefully tore the

paper away to reveal a black velvet jeweler's case. Silence filled the bunkhouse and all eyes remained riveted on the object in Maria's hands. With shaking fingers, she popped open the lid. The breath in her lungs escaped in a loud whoosh. The most beautiful diamond solitaire she'd ever seen glittered and sparkled beneath the room lights.

Wedged inside the box was a tiny note. Maria unfolded the paper and read out loud. "If you trust me with your heart, wear this ring and meet me in Vegas."

Victor tugged Maria's sweater sleeve. "Does Riley want to marry you?"

"No kidding, dumb-ass. That's an engagement ring," Cruz said.

"Are you gonna marry Riley, Ms. Alvarez?" Alonso asked.

Tears burning her eyes, Maria smiled. "As a matter of fact, I am." She slid the ring over her finger and the room erupted in applause.

"HEY, FITZGERALD, DON'T BLOW it tonight!"

Riley scanned the cowboy-ready area at the Thomas and Mac Center on the campus of the University of Nevada-Las Vegas. Out of the crowd walked Billy Stover.

"*You* better not blow it tonight, Stover," Riley said. This evening seven world champions would be crowned and Riley, not Stover, would win the saddle-bronc championship—that is if Riley could keep his mind on business and not Maria.

Gil Parker had phoned him the evening of Thanksgiving to tell him Maria had opened her gift and had left the ranch, wearing the diamond engagement ring. Riley anticipated a call from Maria but one never came and he worried that she'd worn the ring home only to have changed her mind later. Fear and anxiety had eaten away at his gut all week but miraculously he'd come out on top each go-round.

He'd receive a great deal of satisfaction if he silenced the naysayers that had followed him around the circuit this year, but more than anything he was ready to put rodeo behind him and move on to bigger and better things—the most important, beginning a new life with Maria.

If Maria refused to marry him she'd find out soon enough that he wasn't a quitter. He'd already begun making plans toward their future together by purchasing an abandoned ranch southwest of Albuquerque. Riley believed he and Maria would make a great team and with a little TLC the ranch would become a safe haven for the at-risk teens in Maria's program. She'd be a fool to walk away from a chance to help more of her students because she was afraid of her feelings for him.

"Stover, quit hassling Fitzgerald," Ed Parker said as he entered the cowboy-ready area.

"You can boss me around when you become a winner, Parker, but not before." Stover stomped off.

"You ready to take home the championship?" Ed asked.

"If I don't win, it won't be because of my horse."

"Heard you drew White Lightning."

The bronc had thrown all but two riders during the finals—Stover and, after tonight, Riley.

"If you don't have the best ride of your life, Stover's going to edge you out," Ed said.

"Not a chance."

"I do admire your cockiness." Ed grinned. "Dad

said you proposed to that schoolteacher over Thanksgiving."

"How come you weren't at the Gateway Ranch for the holiday?" Riley asked, changing the subject.

"I was in California visiting my little girl." Ed stuck a pinch of chew between his lip and gum. "Win or lose, you gonna retire after tonight, settle down and play house?"

"Yep. What about you?"

"What else am I gonna do if I quit? I sure don't want to punch cows for my old man."

"Would you work for me?" Riley asked.

"Doing what?"

"I'm going to start up a rodeo program for teenage boys who've dropped out of high school. I'll need a few rodeo cowboys on hand to teach the kids." The idea was ambitious, but Riley's trust fund would cover the initial investments and he had a few fundraising ideas to keep the ranch open year-after-year. Riley's father had expressed interest in investing in the program and using the publicity to draw attention to Belle Farms.

Riley's parents and sister had arrived earlier in the week and when he'd explained his intention to marry Maria after his final ride tonight his mother had almost fainted. But after spending several days with Riley and listening to his plans for the future and the role Maria played in those plans his parents had accepted the fact that their son was in love with an older woman.

"When you get the ranch up and running give me a shout. I'll drop by for a look-see," Parker said. "Sure would be nice to settle in one place for a spell. Maybe I'd get to see my daughter more often." Ed tipped his hat. "Good luck tonight."

Riley inched closer to White Lightning's stall. The

rodeo workers had loaded the gelding into the chute a few minutes ago and the animal acted jittery. Riley hoped by the time the chute door opened the bronc would be pissed as hell and ready to rock 'n' roll. He rummaged through his gear bag and put on his chaps, spurs and riding glove.

Focus, damn it. Riley blocked out the noise around him, willing his mind to empty of all thoughts but White Lightning—fat chance.

"Riley!"

Cruz, Alonso and Victor rushed toward him. Frantically he searched for Maria. She stood off to the side, her hands stuffed into the pockets of her jeans. Was she wearing his ring or not?

"Glad you guys made it," Riley said, his attention riveted on Maria.

"A dude in the stands says you drew the best horse," Alonso said.

"I sure did. He's right here." Riley pointed to White Lightning.

"Good luck, Riley. I hope you win." Cruz bumped knuckles with Riley, then he and the other boys walked off. Maria edged closer.

God, he'd missed her.

"You came." *Dumb-ass. Tell her you love her.*

"I'm sorry," she whispered.

"For what?"

"For being a coward."

Her confession surprised him. "You're one of the bravest women I know." *Except when it comes to love.*

"I let my fears dictate my actions when I should have listened to my heart."

Speaking of hearts, Riley's was racing. "What's your heart saying now?"

She pulled her left hand from her pocket and raised it high in the air, where the arena lights bounced off the diamond solitaire. "It's telling me to take a chance on you, Riley."

"You don't have to take a chance on me, honey. I'm the real deal." Riley tugged her closer.

"You're the first man who's come into my life and challenged me to seek my own happiness. To forgive myself for the role I played in my brother's death. To not be afraid of the future. To live in the moment."

"Is that what you're doing now—living in the moment? 'Cause if it is that's not good enough for me." He pressed his palm to her lower back, exerting enough pressure to close the gap between their bodies. Her breasts bumped his chest and Riley swore her heart thumped as hard as his. "I don't want to live moment-by-moment with you. I want forever with you. Maria, I love you with all my heart."

"I'm not going to change my mind about children."

"We don't need to make a decision about having a family anytime soon."

"If I still say no?"

"I can live with that. It's you I can't live without."

"What about your parents? I'm not the woman they would have chosen for you."

"They're coming around. They understand that you're the inspiration for all I want to be in life."

"I don't know if I can ever leave Albuquerque."

"You won't have to."

"You're okay with living in New Mexico?"

"It's where we both belong. Where we can do the most good."

Maria smiled. "You're very wise for a young man, Riley."

"'Bout time you noticed."

"Are you sure?" she asked.

"Only when it comes to you, me and our love."

Her eyes glittered with tears. "I do love you, Riley. I'm glad you made me see the light."

"I'd have fought for your love forever if that's what it took to make you admit that we belong together."

"Really?"

"Yeah, really." Riley kissed her—a teasing, fleeting brush of his lips that left her moaning for more when he pulled away.

"Ladies and gentlemen, it's time to begin the last night of the National Finals Rodeo here at the Thomas and Mac Center in Las Vegas, Nevada!"

Riley ducked his head and spoke in Maria's ear. "I've got our future all mapped out, honey. You hang on to my saddle and I promise you it'll be a hell of a ride."

Ignoring the cowboys who'd gathered around Riley's chute, Maria planted a big wet kiss on his mouth. Wolf whistles echoed through the cowboy-ready area. "Win this one for all the boys out there who dream of being you." Maria kissed him one more time then sashayed away.

"Before we kick off the bronc-bustin' competition, let's give a round of applause to our judges...."

The announcer's voice faded in Riley's head as he struggled to tamp down his excitement at Maria finally accepting his love for her. Turning his thoughts to White Lightning took more strength than Riley anticipated.

"Do-or-die time, big fella." He glanced out of the corner of his eye and watched Stover pace nervously in front of his bronc's chute. He'd drawn Bull's-eye—a horse known for throwing its riders into the rails.

Right then Stover glanced his way and Riley sent him a silent message. *This is my moment, Stover, not yours.*

"Well, folks, it's down to the final two rides of the season here in Vegas." The crowd applauded. "Billy Stover from Waco, Texas, is going to try and tame Bull's-eye. He needs a good score to build a lead over Fitzgerald, the reigning saddle-bronc champion."

Riley retreated to the shadows to watch Stover's ride. The damned cowboy took forever to find his seat in the saddle but once the chute door opened and Bull's-eye bolted for freedom, Stover was in the battle of his life. Bull's-eye was more of a spinner than a bucker, making it difficult for the cowboy to spur. If Stover didn't force the bronc out of his spin he was going to lose valuable points.

The buzzer rang and it was no surprise that Stover had kept his seat—the man rarely got thrown. "Let's see what the judges think of Stover's ride…eighty-two!" The applause was lukewarm at best.

Riley needed an eighty-four to win. "Okay, White Lightning. It's me and you and a date with destiny." Riley climbed the chute rails and slid low in the saddle, then worked his gloved hand around the rope.

"Folks, Riley Fitzgerald's had a rocky run at the title this season. He's been in and out of the standings more times than I can count, but he made it back to Vegas this year and he's vying for a repeat title." Music blared over the loudspeakers and snippets of Riley riding in last year's finals flashed across the Jumbotron.

Win it for the boys. Maria's voice blocked out the noise around Riley.

A world title would lend respect to the rodeo program Riley wanted to establish for troubled teens. A title might also bring in lucrative sponsorship offers. More than a gold buckle rested on this one ride. Riley couldn't afford to fail.

"Chute number seven is where tonight's final action takes place. Riley Fitzgerald from Lexington, Kentucky, is gonna tame White Lightning."

A few more words from the announcer and Riley's date with destiny arrived. The chute door opened and White Lightning leapt for freedom.

Riley's body was pumped full with adrenaline and he had no trouble keeping his spurs above the points of the horse's shoulders. The gelding performed beautifully, throwing its body into buck after buck. The stands blurred before Riley's eyes. As if he and White Lightning were one body, Riley rode out the bucks, keeping his hand high above his head.

When the buzzer sounded, Riley continued to ride, knowing once he got off the horse that would be the end of his career. White Lightning must have sensed Riley's emotions because the horse kept bucking, challenging Riley.

Satisfied he'd done his best on White Lightning, Riley flung his leg over the saddle and leapt for the ground, stumbling twice before regaining his balance.

The crowd stood on its feet, stomping and cheering. The Jumbotron replayed Riley's ride as the announcer said, "Folks, I do believe Riley Fitzgerald settled the debate—he is the reigning saddle-bronc champion of the world! We'll have to wait for next year to see if Fitzgerald can capture a third title."

Not a chance. Riley slipped into the cowboy-ready area and came face-to-face with Maria, the boys, her parents and Riley's family. His throat swelled with emotion. Everyone that mattered most to him was present to help close one chapter of his life and open the next.

He gathered Maria in a hug. "I love you, Maria. Will you marry me tonight?"

Maria's eyes shone with tears. "I love you, too, Riley. And, yes, I'll marry you tonight."

The coliseum crowd roared with approval after witnessing Riley's proposal on the Jumbotron. He kissed Maria, fueling the fans response.

"Fitzgerald got lucky twice tonight, folks—he's not only a world-champion cowboy, he's caught himself a world-champion bride!" the announcer chuckled.

"Good thing you said yes because Elvis is waiting to marry us." Riley ignored his mother's shocked expression. "C'mon, everybody. We've got less than an hour to get to the chapel I booked for our wedding."

Riley's mother gasped. "We haven't sent out announcements! Or decided on colors and flowers and what about the rehearsal dinner?"

"I don't know about you—" Riley gazed into Maria's eyes "—but I sure don't need to rehearse. I'm ready for the real thing."

"Me, too."

"Everyone who means the most to Maria and I are here right now." Riley addressed Maria's parents. "Mr. and Mrs. Alvarez, I know I'm not the man you would have picked for your daughter. But I am the man who will love her and honor her and treat her with all the respect and dignity she deserves."

Ricardo cleared his throat. "That's all a father can ask for. Be happy together."

"Ready?" Riley asked Maria.

Maria giggled. "Viva Las Vegas!"

"I CAN'T BELIEVE YOU BOUGHT this place, Riley," Maria said Christmas morning when Riley stepped onto the porch of the run-down ranch house outside Albuquerque. They'd spent Christmas Eve at her parents' home, where they'd opened gifts. Riley's present to her had been the key that had unlocked the front door of this ranch house.

He slipped a jacket over her shoulders to ward off the chilly morning air. "Five hundred acres of second chances." Riley wrapped his arms around Maria and pointed to the east where a crumbling barn sat. "We'll replace the barn with a new one and fill it with horses. Then add corrals and a bunkhouse." His finger moved west. "We'll string a fence for bucking stock out there."

Maria leaned into Riley, content to listen to his ramblings about improving the property. With the sun rising in the east, casting a pink glow across the morning sky, Maria had found her paradise. She envisioned the hustle and bustle of teenagers doing ranch chores, studying for GEDs and learning that a brighter future was within their grasp if they stayed out of trouble and worked hard.

"Over there, we'll build your classroom and install the latest technology and computers to help with homework."

"I vote we put a new roof on our house first," Maria said. They'd slept in their clothes on the living room floor Christmas Eve and stared at the stars visible through the holes. She faced Riley, wrapping her arms around his neck. "I've decided on a name for the ranch." Riley had given Maria the honor of choosing the name.

"What is it?"

"Riley Fitzgerald Ranch for Boys."

"No way. That's a dumb name, Maria."

"It is not!" She snuggled her head against his chest. "You're the best thing that's ever happened to me. Let me be reminded of how lucky I am each time I answer the phone 'Riley Fitzgerald Ranch for Boys.'"

"I thought you'd name the place after your brother," Riley said.

Caught off guard by the suggestion, Maria blinked back tears.

"Juan Alvarez Ranch for Boys," Riley said.

Maria pressed a soft kiss to Riley's mouth. Long. Slow. Sweet.

He broke off their kiss and said, "Looks like the cavalry has arrived." A caravan of trucks and construction equipment wound their way along the ranch road.

"What's going on?" Maria asked.

"This is our first Christmas at the Juan Alvarez Ranch for Boys and I wanted it to be memorable. We're having a barn-raising today."

"But it's Christmas. Who works on Christmas day?"

Riley grinned. "Money talks."

"You shouldn't have. This must be costing you a fortune, Riley."

"*Us* a fortune. When it comes to making you happy, Maria, money is no obstacle. Now stop worrying. The cowboys are from the Gateway Ranch. Pete's bringing the chuck wagon and he's cooking Christmas barbecue for everyone. My parents are flying in later today and your folks are picking them up at the airport and driving them out here. Cruz, Victor and Alonso and their families are coming, too."

Tears burned Maria's eyes. "This is really happening, isn't it?"

Riley placed her palm against his heart. "Merry Christmas, darlin'."

"I love you, Riley."

"I know. Now let's go welcome everyone to our new home and you can help Pete set up the chuck wagon."

"Sounds like a plan. And, Riley…?"

"What?"

She'd been thinking a lot these past weeks about having a baby with Riley. She was still scared, but not as scared now that she knew they'd raise their child on a ranch and not in the 'hood.

"Never mind." She smiled, tucking her secret away. Once life settled down a bit and the ranch opened its doors to at-risk teens, Maria would discuss starting a family. Or better yet, maybe she'd wait and surprise Riley a few months later with the good news. Right now Maria intended to enjoy every single second with the man who showed her that real-life heroes really do exist.

* * * * *

HEART & HOME

Heartwarming romances where love can
happen right when you least expect it.

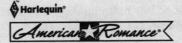

COMING NEXT MONTH
AVAILABLE JANUARY 10, 2012

#1385 HIS VALENTINE TRIPLETS
Callahan Cowboys
Tina Leonard

#1386 THE COWBOY'S SECRET SON
The Teagues of Texas
Trish Milburn

#1387 THE SEAL'S PROMISE
Undercover Heroes
Rebecca Winters

#1388 CLAIMED BY A COWBOY
Hill Country Heroes
Tanya Michaels

REQUEST YOUR FREE BOOKS!
2 FREE NOVELS PLUS 2 FREE GIFTS!

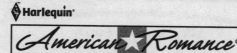

Harlequin®

American Romance®

LOVE, HOME & HAPPINESS

YES! Please send me 2 FREE Harlequin® American Romance® novels and my 2 FREE gifts (gifts are worth about $10). After receiving them, if I don't wish to receive any more books, I can return the shipping statement marked "cancel." If I don't cancel, I will receive 4 brand-new novels every month and be billed just $4.49 per book in the U.S. or $5.24 per book in Canada. That's a saving of at least 14% off the cover price! It's quite a bargain! Shipping and handling is just 50¢ per book in the U.S. and 75¢ per book in Canada.* I understand that accepting the 2 free books and gifts places me under no obligation to buy anything. I can always return a shipment and cancel at any time. Even if I never buy another book, the two free books and gifts are mine to keep forever.

154/354 HDN FEP2

Name	(PLEASE PRINT)

Address	Apt. #

City	State/Prov.	Zip/Postal Code

Signature (if under 18, a parent or guardian must sign)

Mail to the **Reader Service:**
IN U.S.A.: P.O. Box 1867, Buffalo, NY 14240-1867
IN CANADA: P.O. Box 609, Fort Erie, Ontario L2A 5X3

Not valid for current subscribers to Harlequin American Romance books.

Want to try two free books from another line?
Call 1-800-873-8635 or visit www.ReaderService.com.

* Terms and prices subject to change without notice. Prices do not include applicable taxes. Sales tax applicable in N.Y. Canadian residents will be charged applicable taxes. Offer not valid in Quebec. This offer is limited to one order per household. All orders subject to credit approval. Credit or debit balances in a customer's account(s) may be offset by any other outstanding balance owed by or to the customer. Please allow 4 to 6 weeks for delivery. Offer available while quantities last.

Your Privacy—The Reader Service is committed to protecting your privacy. Our Privacy Policy is available online at www.ReaderService.com or upon request from the Reader Service.

We make a portion of our mailing list available to reputable third parties that offer products we believe may interest you. If you prefer that we not exchange your name with third parties, or if you wish to clarify or modify your communication preferences, please visit us at www.ReaderService.com/consumerschoice or write to us at Reader Service Preference Service, P.O. Box 9062, Buffalo, NY 14269. Include your complete name and address.

SPECIAL EDITION

Life, Love and Family

Karen Templeton

introduces

The FORTUNES *of* TEXAS: Whirlwind Romance

When a tornado destroys Red Rock, Texas,
Christina Hastings finds herself trapped in the
rubble with telecommunications heir
Scott Fortune. He's handsome, smart and
everything Christina has learned to guard herself
against. As they await rescue, an unlikely attraction
forms between the two and Scott soon finds
himself wanting to know about this mysterious
beauty. But can he catch Christina before she runs
away from her true feelings?

FORTUNE'S CINDERELLA

Available December 27th wherever books are sold!

www.Harlequin.com

Brittany Grayson survived a horrible ordeal at the hands of a serial killer known as The Professional... who's after her now?

Harlequin® Romantic Suspense presents a new installment in Carla Cassidy's reader-favorite miniseries, LAWMEN OF BLACK ROCK.

Enjoy a sneak peek of **TOOL BELT DEFENDER.**

Available January 2012 from Harlequin® Romantic Suspense.

"**B**rittany?" His voice was deep and pleasant and made her realize she'd been staring at him openmouthed through the screen door.

"Yes, I'm Brittany and you must be..." Her mind suddenly went blank.

"Alex. Alex Crawford, Chad's friend. You called him about a deck?"

As she unlocked the screen, she realized she wasn't quite ready yet to allow a stranger inside, especially a male stranger.

"Yes, I did. It's nice to meet you, Alex. Let's walk around back and I'll show you what I have in mind," she said. She frowned as she realized there was no car in her driveway. "Did you walk here?" she asked.

His eyes were a warm blue that stood out against his tanned face and was complemented by his slightly shaggy dark hair. "I live three doors up." He pointed up the street to the Walker home that had been on the market for a while.

"How long have you lived there?"

"I moved in about six weeks ago," he replied as they

walked around the side of the house.

That explained why she didn't know the Walkers had moved out and Mr. Hard Body had moved in. Six weeks ago she'd still been living at her brother Benjamin's house trying to heal from the trauma she'd lived through.

As they reached the backyard she motioned toward the broken brick patio just outside the back door. "What I'd like is a wooden deck big enough to hold a barbecue pit and an umbrella table and, of course, lots of people."

He nodded and pulled a tape measure from his tool belt. "An outdoor entertainment area," he said.

"Exactly," she replied and watched as he began to walk the site. The last thing Brittany had wanted to think about over the past eight months of her life was men. But looking at Alex Crawford definitely gave her a slight flutter of pure feminine pleasure.

*Will Brittany be able to heal in the arms of Alex,
her hotter-than-sin handyman...or will a second
psychopath silence her forever? Find out in*
TOOL BELT DEFENDER
*Available January 2012
from Harlequin® Romantic Suspense
wherever books are sold.*